The Cat That Ate a Thousand Bananas

Musings of a Nerd

Hank Mancini

The Cat That Ate a Thousand Bananas

Copyright © 2019 by Hank Mancini

All rights reserved. No part of this book may be reproduced or transmitted in any form or by any means without written permission of the author.

Connect with the author at: catatebananas.com

Acknowledgments

Most books have a page or two with acknowledgments, so I have included one too. But rather than simply acknowledge, I have many to thank, beginning with my parents.

My mom, Dolores (Dee), and my dad Arminio (aka Tuff and Joe) are, and have always been, wonderful parents. The best! They allowed me the freedom to be weird and screw-up as often as I wanted to! Thanks, mom and dad!

Thanks to my wife Teresa for her love and for allowing me to spend hours and hours in my office writing this thing!

Thanks to my former wives Stacia and Phyllis, who put up with my immaturity and are the mothers of four of my six wonderful children.

A big "thank you" to my mentors and friends who are, as you read, a large part of this story.

Finally, I thank Jenn Bailey, who edited my unruly manuscript, turning it into a much more readable document.

Table of Contents

You Don't Have to Read This Book 1
The Whys 3
il Buono, il Brutto, il Cattivo 5
The Cat 7
Don't Call Me Dude 9
Digressions 11
My First Job 13
The Iceman Cometh 15
Potato Chips 17
Don't Play with Matches 19
Free Candy 21
Penny Postcards 23
Academic Honors 25
Shooting my First Deer 27
De Happiest Place on de Earth, Mon! 31
Proud to be a Nerd 33
I Did It 35
A Hundred Miles 37
Keeping Score 41
The Key to My Success 43
Newborn Babies All Look Alike 47
Big Spenders 51
Staff and Students Snub Ceremony 53
Age Discrimination 57
Thank You Edwin Land 59

Looking for Love (in All the Wrong Places) 61

Phoenix, Alaska? 63

I Didn't Do It! 65

It Was There This Morning 67

The Bank Deposit 69

Goliath 73

Doing Donuts in a Parking Lot 77

It Was a Mad Mad Mad Mad World 79

My Girlfriend Would Have Been Impressed 81

The Summer of '64 83

Of Course, We Fix Lamps 87

A Hundred Dollar Bet! 89

We're Going the Wrong Way 91

An Afternoon Gone Bad 95

I Thought I Was Going to Maine! 97

A Package of Napkins 101

The Amazing Race 105

Climate Change 107

Deja Vu 109

A Toothache 111

The World Had Changed 113

'65 Mustang 115

Grasshoppers 119

NOIBN 121

Learning to Shoot Craps 123

New Year's Eve in Vegas 127

I Do It Myself 131

Working Late 133

Short Vegas Vacation	135
310 Termino	139
Christmas	143
Dr. Z	145
Dirty Pictures	149
The Building is Tilting!	151
Picking Up Girls	155
Picking Up Girls – Part 2	159
Clean Toilets	161
Holiday Inn	163
Brand Loyalty	167
The Art of Negotiation	169
Christmas II	171
A Bag of Cash	173
Girl Scout Days	175
My Valet	177
The Big Fight	179
BF II	181
Cold Turkey	183
Crumb Cake Marinara	185
Executive Privilege	187
51 and 0	189
Payback	193
Choosing the Wrong Door	195
Laziness Paid Off	197
Karaoke Nights	199
Mr. Behr	203
Vestirsi Come un Italiano	205

Greed	207
Another Bag of Cash	209
The Colonoscopy	213
He Took Us to a Dump	215
2,611 Miles	217
The Most Difficult Time	219
Sirens All the Way	225
Choosing the Wrong Door…Again	227
Swallowing a Stick	229
The End	231

You Don't Have to Read This Book

Writing this paragraph, I cannot imagine many, outside of my family, picking up this book and reading it! But, if you have, you may be wondering what this book is about. It is not about a cat that was really into eating bananas! (More about that later.)

The stories in this book are about events in my life that I remember as humorous or amusing. No one else may think they are.

The happenings in this book are as I remember them. If anyone else remembers them differently, that's their prerogative. Have I embellished? Very likely.

This is not the story of my life. If it were, it would be much longer, and even I would get bored reading it.

No one reading this book must read it! If you start, but for any reason want to stop...stop. I won't be offended.

The Whys

You may be wondering why I am doing this—writing a book about some of the events in my life. There are several reasons, and possibly one of the following may make sense:

1. My kids, grandkids, or even my wives (don't worry, I only had one wife at a time) might get a laugh from reading about these situations and events.
2. By writing this, I have an opportunity to thank the many people who have helped make my life happy, by putting up with my silliness, crazy antics, and occasional pranks.
3. No one else will write about me. I have not done anything—either good or bad—that is significant enough for anyone to write about.
4. No one else knows these events with the same depth of detail that I do.
5. Well, there really isn't a fifth reason, but doesn't five reasons sound better than four?

I have never written a book before. This is my first, and very likely, last.

il Buono, il Brutto, il Cattivo

Clint Eastwood's film career really took off after he starred in Sergio Leone's Dollars Trilogy, a string of Spaghetti Westerns that culminated with, "Il Buono, il Brutto, il Cattivo" (The Good, the Bad, and the Ugly) in 1966. This book has no connection to that film whatsoever. Except in the title of this chapter.

In the film, Leone explored the good, the bad, and the ugly lives of his characters played by Clint Eastwood, Lee Van Cleef, and Eli Wallach. In my book, I am only going to explore and write about the good! None of the bad or ugly experiences of my life will be included. Truthfully, there have been very few instances of anything unpleasant. I have been extremely fortunate to have had a life filled with good. The few bad situations in my life were all my own doing, and I will not dwell on those.

Have I done wrong? Of course! Have I made mistakes? Way, way too many to list. Do I regret things that I have done? Oh yes! Are any of these things going to be included in this book? Probably not. That is one of the advantages of writing about your own life. Someone else writing about me would likely include the unsavory parts, and that would paint a much different picture of me than the one I will paint for you.

The Cat

What kind of cat would eat so many bananas?

Well, to be honest, there is no cat that plays a role in this story. Years ago, when I first started writing some of the good stories of my life, the title just popped into my head.

Throughout the years, we have had quite a few cats. Never once have I known one of our cats, let alone any cat, to eat a single banana. But I liked the title. It has stayed with me for several decades, so here it is!

Possibly, a group of people...cat lovers...might be tricked into reading this story based on the title. I guess that might be considered dishonest on my part. Forgive me.

Don't Call Me Dude

My full and legal name is Armen Nicholas Mancini, but since high school, I have gone by Hank. When someone sees both names and asks what they should call me, I reply you can call me anything, but don't call me Dude!

Some of my aversion to being called Dude stems from the nickname "Doody" that my father gave me when I was very young. At the time, "The Howdy Doody Show" was a very popular children's TV program. Howdy Doody was the puppet star of the show along with Buffalo Bob and Clarabelle the clown.

Several of my high school friends thought I needed a name other than Armen. A few called me Zuke, short for Zucchini (because I was Italian, and Zucchini is an often thought of as an Italian vegetable). A few others called me Hank, which is short for Henry. At the time, Henry Mancini's "Mr. Lucky" was a big hit. Of the two nicknames, I preferred Hank, and that seemed to stick.

Now, back to why I don't want to be called Dude.

There is only one Dude, and that is the character Jeffrey "The Dude" Lebowski, played by Jeff Bridges in the 1998 film "The Big Lebowski." To call me, or anyone else Dude dishonors a great movie.

Digressions

di·gress – verb – to leave the main subject temporarily in speech or writing.

So that you might better understand why I did what I did, I often stray from the story I am telling to explain how things were 30, 40, 50, or even 60 years ago.

My nine-year-old granddaughter did not believe me when I told her there was no Instagram when she was born, and no Facebook when her aunts and uncles (my kids) were growing up.

"How did they know what their friends were doing?" she asked.

Things were a lot different when I was growing up in the '50s and '60s! My digressions may help younger readers understand the situations I was in a little better.

My First Job

Every story has a beginning, and I guess that this story begins the day I was born. It was Friday, October 12th, 1945, the real Columbus Day! I was born in Warren, Ohio, when my mother and father were both 17 years old. Yikes!

My first child, Christopher, was born when I was 25, and I was too young to be the type of father that I would want. I am sorry, Chris. You were the first, and I had no training or experience being a father when you were born.

How did my teenage parents manage their relationship with each other and do a great job of raising my brother, Jim, and me? I don't know. Perhaps it was just what young parents did after living through the war years.

My grandmother, Virginia Reiger, died about two weeks after I was born, and I am not sure if she ever met me. The person that I considered my grandma was my great-grandmother Alice Ellingsworth née Harmison. (FYI, née means, originally called.) We called her "Mammy," and she was a wonderful and loving grandma.

Much of our family on my mother's side lived above a bar and pool hall on Main Street in Warren. I remember that I could hang out the front window and see everything happening on the busy street below. My great grandmother lived in the front apartment and her brother Leo Harmison lived in a connecting apartment. I called him uncle Leo, but he was my great, great uncle.

I don't remember my uncle having a regular job. He would have been 66 years old when I was five, so he was probably retired. I think he had been a painter—the house type not the artistic type—although he may have painted houses in an artistic manner.

His amazing skill was being able to fix complicated things like watches and clocks. I wanted to do this too, but being only five or six years old, I was just too young. I would take apart big clocks that he gave me and end up with a pile of gears, springs, screws, and no idea of how to put them back together. But it was still fun, especially if I was "working" alongside my uncle.

Directly across the street from my grandma's apartment was a place called The Craft Shop. I don't know why it was called The Craft Shop because the store had nothing to do with any crafts. The place sold cigarettes, cigars, chewin' tobacco, and magazines.

When I would go to The Craft Shop with my uncle, I would get to sweep the floor out front while my uncle "had business" in the back; something to do with "The Numbers."

Leo Harmison – my great, great uncle

Sweeping the floor earned me a piece of candy and kept me busy, which I think was the point.

My first job was sweeping the floor of a tobacco shop! I have never put this on a resume but am rethinking that decision.

The Iceman Cometh

How many times have you done something that you regret? This chapter is about the first memory that I have of regretting something that I did.

If you have seen either the Eugene O'Neill play, "The Iceman Cometh," or the 1973 movie of the same name, you may think you know what direction this story will take. Sorry. The iceman that I am writing about was the one who hauled a hundred-pound block of ice up the stairs to the second floor.

Before there were refrigerators, there were Ice Boxes. These appliances looked like today's refrigerators but with no electrical/mechanical refrigeration mechanisms. One of the upsides, no electric bill. But, one of the downsides was no little light bulb to come on when the door was opened. It was dark inside an ice box.

To keep things cold, or at least cool, a large block of ice was put into the ice box. As the block of ice melted, you had to (1) replenish the ice, or your stuff would get warm and (2) drain the ice pan (a pan under the ice box that collected the melted ice water. If you forgot to empty the ice pan, you wound up with a big puddle on the floor.

Ice is heavy. Very heavy. A cubic foot of ice weighs more than 50 pounds. Too much for most people to lug around, especially if they live upstairs and there is no elevator! Before electric refrigerators were common, the iceman delivered ice to your home and lugged it to your ice box. Everyone who had an ice box knew when the iceman would come. The question was...how much ice would you get?

I believe that I was five or six years old when I pulled this prank.

The year was 1950-1951. We had a refrigerator at home, and my father's Italian parents had a refrigerator even though his mother called it an "issa boxxa." My great grandmother was poor and that was probably why she still had an ice box.

I remember looking down from my great grandmother's secondfloor apartment and seeing the ice truck coming down the street. To let the iceman know how much ice was needed, everyone with an ice box had a square sign with the numbers 25, 50, 75, and 100 on each of the four edges. The sign was put in a window that the iceman could see it. The number up at the top was how many pounds of ice you wanted delivered.

I don't remember how many pounds my great grandmother wanted, but it was probably 25 or 50. For the first prank of my life, I decided to turn the sign so that 100 was at the top.

Watching out the second story window, I saw the ice truck pull up and saw the iceman look up at the sign in the window. I don't know whether he was surprised by the amount, but after he hauled 100 pounds of ice up the stairs and into my great grandmother's apartment, she was the one who was surprised.

As my great grandmother and the iceman argued, I did my best to become invisible by hiding behind the couch. The iceman grumpily left with half the ice he had hauled up the stairs. I don't know if my great grandmother suspected that I had turned the sign to 100 or not, but I wasn't punished.

I thought it would be fun to see the iceman haul 100 pounds of ice up to my great grandmother's apartment. It wasn't. Even though I wasn't punished, I regretted what I had done. I would have felt better if my great grandmother had punished me!

Potato Chips

Can I interest you in a story about a bag of potato chips? If not, skip to the next chapter.

Growing up, we lived on Drexel Avenue in Warren, Ohio. I think we lived there from the time I was five until we moved to California when I was 12—a big chunk of my formative years. The closest store to our house was about a half-mile away on Parkman Road. It was about a 10-minute walk. On some summer days, when I was out of school, I would make the trip to Parkman Road several times a day. It was no big deal.

I don't remember how old I was or what the circumstances were, but one day, my mom asked me to go to the store and get her a bag of potato chips. I also don't remember why I didn't want to do this. Possibly I was being defiant or perhaps I had something important to do like reading Mad magazine. Whatever the reason, I resisted until I was TOLD to go to the store and bring back a large (10 cents, if I remember correctly) bag of potato chips.

Resigning myself to the inevitable, I finally obeyed because I knew that if I didn't I would have to answer to my dad when he got home from work. My dad worked hard at the local steel mill, and he was tired when he finished work. When he got home, he was not in the mood for dealing with a discipline issue. So, the lesser of two evils was to go to the store and get my mom the potato chips rather than face my dad that evening.

I got to the store, bought the bag of potato chips, and started walking back home, but I was mad. To vent my anger, I started squeezing the unopened bag. During my ten-minute walk home, I turned the chips into a pile of salt and potato sand at the bottom of the unopened bag. Expecting a bag of chips, my mother did not appreciate this at all.

When I heard my Father get home from work, I went down to the basement without being told and waited for the inevitable. I am sure that after a full day at work, the last thing he wanted to do was discipline me (aka spank me), but I deserved it, and he did.

My dad reinforced a valuable lesson: do what your mother says!

Don't Play with Matches

I clearly remember both my mother and father telling me, "Don't play with matches." There was no question in my mind about this. Playing with matches was not something I was allowed to do! I think that you can see where this might be going.

My elementary school was less than a five-minute walk from our house. Directly across the street from the school was a large field with crab apple trees. In the summer, that field was where my friends and I hung out, sometimes for the whole day.

By late summer those small, tart apples were pretty good to eat. Also, by late in the summer, the grass in that field had grown chest-high and was very dry, like straw.

Well, if crab apples tasted good right off the tree, us kids thought they would taste even better if we put them on a stick and roasted them. One of my friends stole some matches from home and, not heading our parents' warning, we started an apple-roasting fire under one of those trees. In hindsight, this was not very smart at all. We were surrounded by dry grass.

Our little fire got out of hand very quickly, and fortunately, we all got away from the flames without being roasted ourselves. I give myself a small amount of credit because I ran straight across the street and pulled the fire alarm on a pole in front of my school.

It seemed like ages, but finally, I heard, then saw five or six firetrucks racing down the street, sirens blaring and lights flashing. I think they thought the school was on fire! I stayed by the alarm, pointing to the field across the street, which was unnecessary because the flames were higher than a house, and thick smoke filled the sky. As the firemen were unrolling their hoses to put out the blaze, one came over to me and asked where I lived. I pointed up the street. He thanked me for reporting the fire and said that I should go straight home.

Starting the fire that burned the field across the street from my school was a significant event in my young life. But to this day, I don't remember what happened afterward! I don't think my mom and dad knew that I had started the fire because I wasn't punished.

You might think that I would have learned a lesson about ignoring my mom and dad's advice. As you read on, you will see that I did not!

Having started a fire accidentally, I realize how dangerous fire can be. When my kids were young, I did my best to make sure that they understood that they shouldn't play with matches!

Free Candy

What kid doesn't love candy?

About a half-mile away from our house, there was a small strip mall. During summer, when school was out, my friends and I would make the trip several times a day, just for something to do.

One of the shops was a drug store. It sold everything that a CVS or Walgreens sells today plus it had a soda fountain! The soda fountain was my favorite place. You could sit on a stool at the counter and get a cherry Coke for five cents, and boy was it great. If you had a dime, you could get an ice cream sundae...chocolate, strawberry, or caramel. Even better, that dime could get you a root beer float in a big frosty glass!

The drugstore always had a large display of boxes of assorted chocolates. Us kids never had the money to buy a box, but we didn't need to. We could buy a full-size candy bar for five cents.

I will digress to explain what some other things cost when I was a kid.

It cost a nickel—five cents—to use a payphone. For those under 30 years old, a payphone was a public phone you would pay to use when you needed to call someone but were not at home. They were all over the place, including one or more in every store and at every gas station. To make a call, you put your nickel in the coin slot at the top. Once you heard the dial tone, you dialed the number. (There were no push-button phones for another 20 years, and cell phones wouldn't be common for more than 40 years.) To ride the bus also cost five cents. A postage stamp was two or three cents, and for that, you could send a letter across the country.

The best deal when I was a kid was going to a movie. A ticket for a kid was a quarter, and you got to see several cartoons and two full-length movies. Two shows for one ticket was called a double-feature, and except for a special film, like "Peter Pan" or "Gone With the Wind," you always got to see a double feature.

OK, back to the story I was starting to tell...where was I? Oh yes, the corner drugstore that sold boxes of candy.

One day, and I don't remember why, we went behind the drug store and rummaged through the trash. To our surprise, we found some unopened one-pound boxes of chocolates. Looking around to make sure no one was watching; we took one of the boxes and ran off.

We got the box open, and sure enough, it was full of assorted chocolates. We each gobbled down a few pieces then quickly ran home, grabbed my wagon, and ran back to the rear of the drugstore. No one was there to see what we were doing so we quickly loaded up my wagon with all the candy in the trash. I think our haul was more than 30 boxes. With the wagon loaded, we headed back to my house.

"Mom...look what we found in the trash at the drugstore!"

My mom, being a whole lot smarter and much more experienced than I was, knew something was not right. "Did you eat any of this candy?" she asked.

"Only a piece or two," I sheepishly replied.

My mom took one of the chocolates from the open box and broke it in half. It was crawling with tiny worms. After I threw up, we took the boxes back to the trash bin behind the drugstore.

You might think that experience would have turned me off candy, but it didn't. I was always looking for a way to get a nickel so I could buy a candy bar.

Penny Postcards

While they were called penny postcards, at the time, they cost two cents. For that, you got a blank postcard to write your message and postage to mail it.

I remember that I was doing poorly in fourth or fifth grade or even both. I am not sure why I was doing so badly, but it caused my mom and dad a lot of grief. It also caused me to suffer consequences that I remember well, to this day.

Wanting my grades to improve, my parents came up with a simple system. They purchased a bunch of penny postcards and addressed them to themselves. They met with my teacher and she agreed to mail one of the postcards every Friday indicating how I had done in class that week.

After reading each postcard, my mom and dad decided whether I would have "privileges" until the next report arrived. Privileges meant hanging out with my friends after school and on weekends and watching TV. I guess that I continued to do poorly in school because I remember that I was not allowed to watch TV for most of the school year.

My favorite show was "The Mickey Mouse Club." Watching it was a big deal to me, and somehow, I came up with the one-dollar membership fee to join the Mickey Mouse Club itself. I was also hooked on a series within the show called "Spin and Marty." The show was about a western summer camp for kids called The Triple R. I still remember some of the lyrics from the theme song:

Way out there at the Triple R
Yippi-yea, Yippi-yo
The horses are the best by far
Yippi-yea, Yippi-yo

That's all the lyrics I remember, but it was a catchy tune for sure!

One of the reasons I was hooked on "Spin and Marty" was because of Annette Funicello. I think most boys my age were in love with her! I don't remember any of the storyline or what her role was, but because of my loss of privileges, I missed seeing her in the weekly episodes.

My mother often felt sorry for me and allowed me to sit on the bottom step going up to my bedroom. I could not see the TV (we didn't get a second TV until 20 years later), but I could hear the TV. Hearing was almost as good as watching TV and it allowed me to keep up on what was happening with Spin, Marty, and Annette at the Triple R.

I am pretty sure my father was not aware of this deception carried out by my mother. Thank you, Mom!

Unlike today, I think that the U.S. Postal Service was profitable in the mid-50s. It could have been because my mom and dad used so many penny postcards trying to get me to stop goofing off in elementary school.

Academic Honors

While pursuing an education, some may receive recognition for their unique achievements. Albert Einstein was recognized for his statistical discussion of atomic behavior, which resulted in a way to calculate the size of atoms. Thomas Edison's scientific successes led to him being made an Officer in the French Legion of Honor (Légion d'honneur) in 1881. Several of my accomplishments have also been recognized, which led to me receiving honors from an educational institution.

One of the achievements that I am most proud of is my Meritorious Award for Milk Boy, earned while I was a student at Emerson Elementary School. I was in fourth or fifth grade when I received this prestigious award.

What did I do to receive this great honor? I delivered small individual bottles of milk to each of the classrooms where they were handed out to students before lunch. (Yes, bottles! In the '50s, milk came in glass bottles, not cartons!) When students arrived at school, those wanting milk would pre-order it, paying five cents for a small bottle. My crucial part of this operation was loading up a cart and delivering the correct number of bottles of white and chocolate milk to each classroom on time.

Another honor earned while an elementary school student at Emerson was a Perfect Attendance certificate. To raise the significance of this award even higher, it states that I was, "neither absent or tardy for the entire 1955-1956 school year."

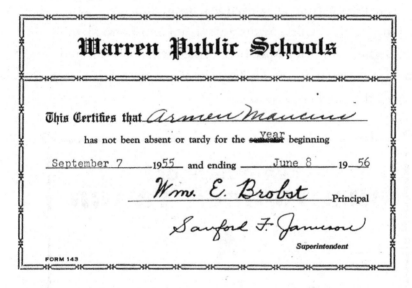

The certificate should have been awarded to my mother. She made sure I went to school every day and got there on time!

Not having a degree from a college or university to hang on my office wall, I have proudly displayed these certificates throughout my career.

Shooting my First Deer

Most parents I know now don't allow their children to play with guns, even toy guns. But when I was young, there was not a single kid that I knew that didn't have at least one toy gun.

Now, I need to clarify what I just said. When I said every kid had a toy guy, I meant every boy. When I was growing up in the early '50s, girls played house with dolls and boys played cowboys and Indians with guns. That was the way it was. I don't think there were any exceptions.

Besides allowing me to play with toy guns, my parents

Me and my "six-shooter"

thought it would be a good idea for me to learn to play the piano. They bought a used upright piano, had it moved into our basement, and paid for me to take weekly piano lessons. In those days, lessons cost $2.00 a week.

I took lessons for three or four years. I learned to read music and "push the keys," but I had no sense of rhythm, so my piano playing never sounded very good. Piano students were required to participate in a once-a-year recital. The song I was to play was "In the Hall of the Mountain King." I don't remember the performance because of what happened just before we left for the event.

The recital was a dress-up affair and my mom had me dressed up and ready to go several hours early. With nothing else to do, I was sitting on our front porch with my toy cap gun. I heard a noise, looked up, and saw a deer running up our street. When it got in front of our house, I did what any kid with a cap gun would do. I took careful aim and shot at the deer several times. The bangs from the cap gun were not very loud, but apparently, the deer saw me and heard my "shots." Startled, it turned away from me, ran into the front yard across the street, and crashed through our neighbor's large plate glass window!

I ran across the street and into our neighbor's house. They were having lunch in their kitchen, and I yelled, "A deer just jumped through your window."

"Someone threw a ball through our window?" our neighbor asked.

"No, a deer just jumped through your front window!" I screamed.

Panicked, the deer had run into a back bedroom and had started bucking and kicking the walls. Our neighbor was able to get the bedroom door closed to trap the deer inside so it would not damage the rest of the house. Not knowing what else to do, someone called the fire department. A reporter from our local newspaper also showed up. A deer jumping through someone's front window seemed to be big news, and an article about the incident and this photo was in the newspaper the next day.

No one could figure out how to get the deer out of the house. It was frightened and had broken the furniture in the bedroom and kicked holes in

the walls. Finally, one of the firemen suggested opening the window. Everyone stood back, and a few minutes later, the deer jumped out the bedroom window and ran off into the woods a few blocks away.

I shot my first and only deer with a cap pistol. Going to the recital was anticlimactic, to say the least.

De Happiest Place on de Earth, Mon!

Before I retired in 2017, people would ask how I would stay busy once I stopped working full time. I often replied that I might get a job at Disneyland, wearing a white uniform, and picking up trash.

Sometimes I daydream, and one of my daydreams is interviewing for a job at Disneyland. I imagine sitting across a desk from a young man and being asked the question: "Why do you want to work at Disneyland?"

In my daydream, I laugh heartily and in a deep baritone voice reply, "You must be kidding me mon. It tis de sign."

The interviewer looks confused. I pause, then add, "De sign. De big sign in de front. It says dis is de Happiest Place on de Earth, Mon."

Of course, I would be hired on-the-spot.

In the summer of 1957, our family drove from Ohio to California in our big Buick sedan for our summer vacation. I don't know if this was only a vacation, or if my parents had thought about moving to California and wanted to check it out. One of my uncles lived in Long Beach and that was our destination.

We saw all the sights and hit all the tourist spots, but the best part of our trip by far was going to Disneyland!

Disneyland was unlike anything I had ever experienced. The rides were amazing. I wanted to drive the Autopia cars all day and ride the Skyway back and forth between Tomorrowland and Fantasyland. (The Skyway closed in 1994, possibly because riders threw stuff on the unsuspecting Disneyland guests below.) I was sad when our day at Disneyland ended, and I think I cried. I didn't want to leave. Knowing that we'd be driving back to Ohio in a few days, I didn't think that I would ever get to see The Magic Kingdom again.

When we traveled, my dad always wanted to get on the road very early. On the morning we were to start driving back to Ohio, I thought it was very unusual that we didn't leave my aunt and uncle's home until after nine. In 1957, there were no freeways in the area, so we took Los Coyotes Diagonal to Willow. Willow turns into Katella, and I remembered that was the way we drove when we went to Disneyland.

Dad surprised us, and it was the best surprise ever. He took us to Disneyland again, and it was wonderful and even more fun the second time.

I still dream about getting a part-time job at Disneyland! If I ever decide to do that, I will practice my Caribbean accent so that I have a better chance of impressing the interviewer and landing my dream job at "De Happiest Place on de Earth, Mon!"

Proud to be a Nerd

After I finished 9th grade, we moved from Long Beach to Lakewood. This was a move of only about three miles.

Late in the summer of 1960, my mom told me she thought that it was time for me to enroll in high school. I walked to Mayfair High School, which to me, was the obvious choice because it was closer than Lakewood High. I signed up for the fall semester...no questions asked. It turned out that I spent three years going to the wrong high school! What a dorky thing to do.

My counselor at Mayfair did not discover (or admit) that I was going to the wrong school until my senior year. Fortunately, I was allowed to stay and graduated from Mayfair High School in 1963.

My senior picture – certainly nerdish!

The school year started after Labor Day and, not wanting to be late, I left home earlier than I needed to. I didn't have a wristwatch, so to keep track of time while I walked to school, I carried an alarm clock. (In the late '50s and early '60s wristwatches were not something that any of the kids that I knew owned. Wristwatches were considered a luxury item and were the gift many kids received when they graduated from high school or even college. It would be another 10 years or so before inexpensive Timex watches became available.)

Not wanting to look like a complete goofball, I carried my alarm clock in my brown paper lunch bag. If I had been less of a nerd, I would not have put the alarm clock on top of my sandwich.

Carrying an alarm clock to school was an early indication that: (1) I was a nerd (and my children will likely confirm that I am still one to this day), and (2) I took (and still take) being on time very seriously.

I am proud that I am a nerd but even prouder that I am a punctual one.

Oh, yes, I got to school on time.

I Did It

I think any other student would likely have gotten into a lot more trouble than I did.

I was sitting in Marshall LaCour's photography class in 10th grade. I don't remember who was sitting next to me, but we were goofing off as the teacher (and someone who would become an important mentor to me) lectured on some aspect of photography.

I tore a sheet of paper out of my notebook, wadded it up in a ball, and pretended like I was going to throw it at the teacher.

"I dare you," said the guy sitting next to me.

Without hesitating, I threw the balled-up wad of paper and hit our teacher on the back of his head as he was writing on the blackboard.

Mr. LaCour jolted in surprise, turned around and barked, "Who did that?"

Raising my hand, I said, "I did."

Mr. LaCour tried not to laugh but couldn't seem to stop himself from doing so. Regaining his composure, he said, "Young man, I'll see you after class."

Disciplinary action was called for, and my penalty was having to stay after school and clean the darkrooms for a week. Most students would

Marshall LaCour – my photo teacher, mentor, and friend

have considered this punishment. It wasn't for me. Because I loved photography, I hung around after school and cleaned the darkrooms almost every day without being asked.

A Hundred Miles

I think that my mom and dad are going to be surprised when they read this. I do not believe they ever knew of my stupid and dangerous escapade in 1961.

Two or three years earlier, my dad, mom, brother Jim, and I drove to San Diego for the day. This was before there was a freeway and the trip took more than three hours. (We still had the big Buick sedan that had brought us from Ohio to California.) For some reason, heading back from San Diego my dad wanted me to drive.

I was not tall enough to safely see over the dashboard, so he sat me on a pillow. I was both thrilled and frightened.

Let me explain first that this was a big car with very wide bench seats. I think five people could sit in the front seat alone. My dad moved over close to the door and had me scoot over next to him so that I could hold the steering wheel, but he could too. Being my very first experience driving, I was having trouble staying in the center of the lane. My dad had to guide the car back to where it was supposed to be until I got the hang of it. What a thrill it was to drive! I think that I was 13 at the time so it would be several years before I could legally drive.

The memory of my first drive stayed with me and as a couple of years passed my desire to drive grew stronger and stronger. Even though we took a lot of day trips, my dad never gave me the opportunity to repeat that wonderful experience.

I'm not sure what happened to the Buick, but my next exciting driving experience was in our powder blue Ford Fairlane. I was in driver's ed after school, had my learner's permit, but had never driven alone.

I've got to tell you something about my dad. He was obsessed with keeping track of his gas mileage. Every time he filled up the tank, he recorded how much gasoline he purchased and the Fairlane's odometer reading. Because of my dad's record keeping, taking his car without him knowing it was going to be very difficult. But I wanted to drive, and I wanted to drive so badly that I devised a plan.

Both my parents were fast asleep by midnight. For a margin of safety, I waited until about 1:00 a.m. before starting my adventure. I took the car keys to the Fairlane and, before I drove off, noted the exact mileage—to the tenth of a mile—and the exact amount of gas in the tank. Then I set out to explore the open roads on my own and enjoy the thrill of driving.

For my nocturnal outing, I decided to drive to Hollywood. At 1:00 a.m. the Long Beach freeway was empty, and I was in downtown Los Angeles in no time. I remember exiting the freeway at Hollywood Boulevard and driving to the corner of Hollywood and Vine. In 1961, this was a sleazy, rundown area, so I didn't linger. It was now about 2:00 a.m., so I headed toward home, driving to Long Beach.

I drove around the deserted streets of downtown Long Beach for a while then decided to head to a McDonald's in Downey. (This was one of the original McDonald's opened by the McDonald brothers. It is the oldest operating McDonald's in the world.) Of course, by the time I got there, it was closed. I was tired and tired of my adventure, so I headed back to Lakewood.

I had planned on adding gas at a station near our home that was open all night, but when I got there, I had only driven 89 miles. I knew that it was only 1.2 miles from the gas station to home, so I had to drive around the neighborhood adding miles to the odometer. I pulled into the gas station having driven 98.8 miles. It took about 8 gallons to get the needle back to where it was when I took my dad's car. The cost amounted to just over $2.00.

Driving down our street and nearing home, I put the car in neutral and turned off the engine. A few moments later I coasted into our driveway, quietly snuck back into the house, and put my dad's keys back where I found them. I was exhausted!

It was about a week before I heard any inkling that something was wrong, but I remember my dad being mad at himself for messing up his mileage log. He figured that he had made a mistake because he could not understand why he got about a hundred extra miles from his last fill-up.

What I did was dangerous and stupid! I was lucky that I got back home safely without having accident or being pulled over by the police or highway patrol. Either would have put an end to my driving for a long, long time.

Mom and Dad, I'm sorry!

Keeping Score

Does my astrological sign affect my life?

Being born on October 12th means that I am a Libra. The sign for Libra is the balance, and I really do like things to be balanced. To achieve balance, you need to keep track of things.

I think this internal need for keeping an accurate track of things is what made me a pretty good bowling scorekeeper.

Bowling was much more popular when I was growing up than it seems to be today. There were more bowling alleys, and they were very busy with league play every evening. Most bowling alleys had early evening and late evening leagues.

The bowling alley closest to home was Cal Bowl on Carson in Long Beach. It was just over 4 ½ miles away. I could walk each way in just over an hour, which is how I got there and back.

Not having a job and wanting spending money I decided to try my hand as a scorekeeper. Because my mom and dad had bowled in leagues, I knew that scorekeepers could earn $2.50 for about two hours of work. There were five players on each of the two teams, and each of the 10 players chipped in 25 cents to pay the scorekeeper.

Keeping score for bowling is simple. Any of the players on either team could have done it except that the players that I kept score for usually drank as they bowled. Interesting how accuracy and fairness can decrease while empty bar glasses increase. Hence, the necessity for a sober (and paid) scorekeeper.

If you wanted to work as a scorekeeper, you showed up about 30 minutes before play was scheduled to start. As team members arrived and put on their bowling gear, I would ask if they needed a scorekeeper. At first, the answer was often, "No, sorry, we have a regular scorekeeper." But a few evenings later, I got my first gig.

In the span of a few weeks, I had kept score for several different teams, and without exception, each had asked me to keep score for them the following week. Most evenings I was earning $5 which, to me, was good money. Because I was a senior in high school, I also had homework to do. The simple solution was to do my homework while keeping score.

When I first opened a schoolbook at the scorer's table, a startled bowler said, "You can't do that. You need to pay attention to the game. This is really important!"

But, they were in the middle of the second of three games, and it was either let me divide my attention or find someone else to keep score. I soon showed that I could do both; keep score accurately and do my homework.

I think I gained respect by showing the bowlers that I considered school to be important. As I kept score for the same teams each week, I started getting questions about school and how I was doing. Possibly some of the bowlers felt sorry for me because they started treating me to a Coke, a piece of pie, or even a burger.

I was also being asked for simple scorekeeping favors such as "marking a fence" (A bold vertical line that will hopefully end bad bowling by one player.) or "circling a turkey." (A turkey is three strikes in a row.) These requests often came with some extra change dropped on the table in front of me! On a particularly good night, I might earn an extra dollar.

Getting a part-time job at Memorial Hospital caused me to end my scorekeeping career, but to this day, I know how to do it! Occasionally, if I am having trouble falling asleep, I dream of keeping score at an imaginary bowling game. I guess that makes me a true Libra.

The Key to My Success

What would you have done if you had been given a key to your high school that unlocked every door?

Of the approximately 1,200 students at Mayfair High School, I am confident that I was the only one that had a master key. I am pretty sure that none of the teachers had a master key, but I did!

A week before I was scheduled to start my senior year at Mayfair, I got a call from Mr. R., my guidance counselor, asking if I would be willing to work and set-up the photo lab. He said that my photo instructor, Mr. LaCour, was sick and could not do his normal pre-semester preparation. I would earn a dollar an hour—minimum wage at the time—and the thanks of both my favorite teacher and the school.

The next day I showed up at the office to meet with Mr. R. He quizzed me to see if I knew what needed to be done—I did—and if I would do it—I would. His next problem was getting me a key to the photo labs and the adjoining classroom. He had keys to neither but wanted me to start right away. He took a key off his key ring, gave it to me, and had me promise to bring it back and exchange it the next day.

"Don't lose this, please," was his only request. Walking over to the photo lab, I noticed the word "MASTER," and the phrase, "DO NOT DUPLICATE" were stamped into the key. Hmm. Very interesting.

I worked all day getting everything in order in two of the darkrooms—I had done this for free during the previous school year—then decided to see what doors this master key would open. Next door to the photo lab was the chemistry lab. Yep, my key opened that door. Across the way was one of the teacher's restrooms. Yes, the key worked on that door too. I checked the teacher's parking lot, and there were no cars left, so I headed to the administration building. Yep, my key opened the main door and the door to the teachers lounge and the door to the principal's office. Holy crap.

So, how did my master key benefit me during my senior year?

The restrooms at Mayfair High School—at least the boy's bathrooms—were neither clean nor private in any way. The stalls had no doors, and it was common if you had to sit to do you stuff that some other kid would be standing there making fun of you. Because of that, I never used the restrooms during breaks. Instead, I got excused during class. But, during my senior year, the master key was my key to a much more civilized bathroom experience.

Between two of the Industrial Arts buildings was a small, out-of-the-way staff restroom and it became my private bathroom. It had a clean urinal, and a toilet stall with a door that not only closed but locked. For the first few weeks I used it, I was afraid that a teacher or other staff member would come in while I was there and that would be the end of my master key privilege. However, I noticed that there was never any trash in the wastepaper can.

I decided to conduct a test to see if the restroom was used by anyone other than me. I dropped a chewed-up piece of gum into the bottom of the toilet bowl. It was not easy to see, and I reasoned that if it were still there the next day, the toilet would not have been flushed or cleaned. The piece of gum was there the next day. I repeated this test the rest of the week and the gum was always there. This told me that the janitor, seeing the restroom unused, didn't even flush the toilet! Throughout my senior year, I don't think anyone else ever used my private bathroom.

My key also let me into the teachers workroom that had a mimeograph machine. A mimeograph machine was how copies were made before there were copy machines. I don't remember what the process was, but the chemicals that the machine used were very pungent. Mimeographed copies had a unique smell that no one from that era would forget, and the copied image was a distinctive blue.

A very cute girl that I was interested in was running for some Junior Class office. As far as I could tell she did not have any chance of winning the election. We were in the photography and biology clubs together, and I really wanted to see more of her. She did not seem all that interested in me so figured that I needed a way to show her what a great guy I was.

One of the things I liked about Stephanie was that she had a great sense of humor. She laughed out loud when I told her I was going to get her elected.

By this time, I was bold about accessing school resources that were usually only available to teachers. The weekend before the election, I got a couple of mimeograph stencils and made up 8 ½ x 11 posters saying, "Vote for Stephanie" and, "Stephanie's the One." Using the teacher workroom late Sunday evening I ran off enough copies to put several in every classroom. I pinned them to the bulletin boards and taped them to the classroom windows.

Monday morning, my campaign signs were unavoidable. They were everywhere. No one ever seemed to question how campaign signs for Stephanie showed up in every classroom on campus. A few days later we voted, and of course, Stephanie easily won whatever she was running for. She laughed as she thanked me and then celebrated by going to the school dance the next Friday night with another guy!

My master key to the school gave me a clean, private restroom, but it did not bring me success with the girl I wanted to date!

Newborn Babies All Look Alike

You may question my statement that newborn babies all look alike but I will explain why I can make that bold statement.

My first steady job was working as a photo lab technician at Long Beach Memorial Hospital—now called Memorial Hospital Medical Center. I worked part-time during my senior year in high school, and after I graduated.

Having a baby was a lot different in 1963 than it is today. I think the biology was about the same, but mothers went into the hospital and did not come out for days. Newborn babies were protected and isolated in the hospital and were only brought to their mothers' rooms for bottle feeding. (I think there was a stigma that only poor women breastfed their babies.) During the brief time babies were with their mothers, no visitors were allowed in the room.

Babies spent most of their time swaddled tightly and lying in clear plastic bassinets in the newborn nursery. They were attended to by nurses wearing white uniforms, white hats, white stockings, and white leather shoes!

While lying in their bassinet in the nursery, a nurse would position a movable camera over the baby and take "Baby's First Photo." This typically happened on the day the baby was born, and no great care was taken to ensure that the photo of the newborn was a good one. Often the baby's eyes were closed, and often they moved their head, so the shot was blurry.

I would start my job by going up to the newborn nursery and scrubbing up like I was going to perform surgery. I had to gown up with booties, mask, and all. A nurse would often watch to make sure that I scrubbed my hands and arms for a full 15 minutes. If I sensed they were not paying attention, I might knock off a few minutes, but I didn't get away with that very often.

Only after being suitably attired...looking like I was going to perform open-heart surgery...was I permitted to enter the newborn nursery and remove the film magazine from the baby camera. This operation typically took less than five minutes, and that included sliding a replacement magazine into the camera and making sure that it worked. With the used film magazine in hand, I went down to the photo lab to perform darkroom magic...or, in other words, do my job.

Doing newborn photos was a great job because I was paid for five hours of work a day regardless of how long it took me. I don't know who came up with the five hours, but it NEVER EVER took me that long. I also liked the flexibility. As long as I had the previous day's work finished by 8:00 a.m. the next morning I was doing my job.

So, what did I do? The first step in the lab was to process the film. The photos were black and white, so developing the film took me about 30 minutes. After I developed the film, I printed the pictures of the newborn babies. The nurses usually shot five or six photos of each baby, and I was responsible for choosing the best one. I printed two 5 x 7 photos, six wallet size photos, and one small keychain photo. I put the 5 x 7s into cardboard folders and die cut the smallest picture for the keychain. I slid everything into an envelope—blue for boys and pink for girls—and wrote the mother's name on the front.

The candy stripers—high school female volunteers dressed in white dresses with...of course...pink stripes—took the photos to each mother's room and the family almost always bought the package. I think the cost was about $8. Sometimes a family did not purchase the photos. Those came back to the photo lab and were kept in case the family changed their mind. The unpurchased photos were stored for three months, so we always had dozens of unsold "Baby's First Photo" packages.

Occasionally, none of the photos that the nurse shot of the newborn were any good. Sometimes the baby was moving, and the picture was blurred, other times the flash did not go off, so the photo was too dark. I was supposed to fill out a card to request that the baby have more photos shot the next day so the family would have a good "Baby's First Photo." Always being interested in efficiency, e.g., the least amount of time to do my job, I personally, and confidentially, developed a much more streamlined and efficient system.

When a newborn's photos were not of acceptable quality, I would go into the files of unsold pictures and, pretty much at random, pull a set of photos of a different baby. I put these into the appropriate envelope, blue or pink, and wrote the parent's name on the front. Not knowing any better, the candy stripers would then present the alternate pictures to the mothers as THEIR baby's first photos. I don't know if it was luck or what, but never once did any anyone ever question whether the substituted photos were their baby or not!

If a parent can't tell their baby from another, that's proof that newborns must all look alike.

Big Spenders

While I was working at Long Beach Memorial Hospital, I would often work evenings or even nights. The only schedule requirement was that I complete my work…producing the packages of "Baby's First Photos" by 8:00 a.m. Often one of my friends would stop by to visit. I'd take a break, and we would get something to eat in the hospital coffee shop.

No, the coffee shop was not a Starbucks! It would be more than 20 years before the first Starbucks store opened in Seattle. (For those under 30, a coffee shop was a casual restaurant with waitresses, an extensive menu, and reasonable prices.) The coffee shop at the hospital was a really good one.

My friends and I would almost always have a hamburger, fries, and chocolate milkshake. I think this trio cost about $2.00, which was two hours pay. Because I was under no time constraints to get back to work, we would often sit and talk after we finished eating. That was until the waitress came over and asked, "Is there was anything else?"

That was a clue that she wanted us to pay and leave.

I'd often say, "Do it again."

"What do you mean?" she would ask.

"Just repeat our order," I would say.

"Are saying you both want another burger, fries, and shake?" she would ask with a great deal of skepticism.

"Yes!"

"What are you guys, Big Spenders? Are you sure you have the money to pay for this?"

LAKEWOOD DAILY NEWS
Some of the News Some of the Time

Thursday January 17th 1963   25 ¢

Staff and Students Snub Ceremony
Lakewood, Jan 16, 1963 — The gala groundbreaking ceremony for Mayfair High School's long-awaited Sub-School 3 was snubbed by staff and students. Event organizer, Hank Mancini said, "Bob and I thought we'd get at least a couple of teachers and a few-dozen students, but none showed up!"

An elaborate ceremony was not planned and Mancini confirmed that the Mayfair High School Marching Band was not asked to play for the event. "We just wanted a few of our favorite teachers and a few friends to show up, but

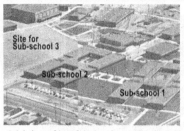

Ariel view of Mayfair showing undeveloped site for Sub-School 3

Car Crashes Into Tree—late Wednesday evening, a car apparently crashed into a large tree at the corner of Main Street and Hazelbrook Avenue

---

Mayfair High School, home of the Monsoons, was unique compared to the other nearby high schools. The school was divided into two "subschools,"—Subschool 1 and Subschool 2. Students were assigned to one of the two subschools for the four years they were at Mayfair. Most required classes were taken within the student's assigned subschool. Elective classes were located on the opposite side of the campus and served students from both.

The concept of subschools was that students would do better, both academically and socially, attending a smaller school. Each of the subschools would serve about 500 students. This was compared to nearby Lakewood High School (where I was supposed to go) with nearly 4,000 students.

More students wound up at Mayfair than had been planned, and classes in both subschools were overflowing. From the time I started at Mayfair, the ground was always about to be broken on Subschool 3. But... during my years there, it never happened.

My good friend Bob and I decided to move things along. One evening we held our own groundbreaking ceremony in the vacant space were Subschool 3 was to be built. It was just Bob holding a shovel, me holding a sign, and a camera set up on a tripod.

Remember, I had a master key to the school, so after I developed and printed an 8 x 10 photo of our ceremony, we put it up on the bulletin board in the teachers lounge.

The next morning, I received a call slip in my English class to see my guidance counselor. I was afraid that I would be reprimanded for tacking up the photo in the teachers lounge. I was even more afraid that it would lead to the realization that I had a master key and that it would be taken away. I waited nervously until he had finished with another student.

"We need your help making a slide show for open house," my counselor said. (The slide show took me a couple of months to complete and was titled, "The Mayfair Story," but that's another story.)

Not only did no one come to our groundbreaking ceremony, but no mention was ever made, nor were any questions asked about how the photo of the mock ceremony wound up hanging on the bulletin board in the teachers lounge!

Our ceremony may have worked because a few years after I graduated, construction final began.

Age Discrimination

In 1967, President Lyndon B. Johnson signed the Age Discrimination in Employment Act into law. The act forbids employment discrimination against anyone at least 40 years old. The act did nothing to help me because I was only 17 when I faced age discrimination and the act would not become law for another 4 years.

As my senior year at Mayfair High School was ending my goal was to get a full-time job. Hopefully, a good-paying job. In the '60s in Southern California, the best jobs were in the aerospace industry at McDonell Douglas and North American Aviation.

My mentor and photo teacher at Mayfair, Mr. LaCour, had a connection at North American Aviation and offered to help me get a job. It was early April when I had my first interview at the sprawling plant in Downey. I was intimidated to interview at such a high-profile company. North American was building spaceships—the Saturn booster and the Apollo Command Module.

I don't remember who I interviewed with or what questions I answered, but after about 15 minutes, I was asked when I could start. I was being offered a job in the photo lab.

I replied, "The Monday after graduation."

The interviewer said, "Great. We deal with classified information, so you'll need to get a security clearance, and that involves a lot of paperwork."

A security clearance. This was even better than I imagined. What kind of things would I be working with and what cool stuff would I get to see? Wow! I was excited!

I arranged to come in and start filling out all the pre-employment paperwork and security clearance forms the next week. There was a lot of paperwork and I was photographed and fingerprinted. It took me all afternoon. Before I left, I was told, "You'll hear from us in three or four weeks."

Those weeks were very long weeks. I received a call.

"Mr. Mancini, can you come in and discuss your application?" said the caller.

Hmm...discuss my application. What did that mean? Had I made a mistake, or had I left some questions unanswered? I thought, OK, that sounded like they wanted to hire me, or they would have told me I didn't get the job over the phone.

I went back to North American in early June and met with a guy who had my paperwork in front of him.

"I am sorry to tell you, Mr. Mancini, because you're not 18 years old. You can't get a security clearance. Without a security clearance, we can't hire you for the photo lab."

I think I was able to hold back tears and remain composed, but I was crushed! My age was keeping me from getting the job I had been dreaming about for months.

"You can apply again in October after you turn 18, and if we have an opening, you'll probably be hired."

Fifty plus years later, sitting here writing about my not getting the job at North American Aviation, I feel very fortunate! I have had an incredible career. I doubt if I would have had such a rewarding professional life if I had gotten that job in the aerospace industry. Age discrimination when I was 17 seems to have benefited me!

Thank You Edwin Land

It is unlikely that any of you reading this recognize the name Edwin Land. But his invention, the Polaroid Land Camera, changed photography forever and helped jump start my career.

Being a healthy 17-year-old guy, I wanted a girlfriend. I hadn't been doing too well on that front and thought that having a car would be a big help. My mom and dad were not in the financial position to help, so my only option was to earn enough money myself. Graduating from high school, I would have more time to work and more time to work would mean money to buy a car.

I was still working part-time at Memorial Hospital doing Baby's First Photos. But getting paid minimum wage—a dollar an hour—for 25 hours a week was just not cutting it. I figured that since my work only took 15 to 18 hours, I had plenty of time for another job.

My high school photo teacher and mentor offered to help again. He called a friend who owned a camera store in Long Beach. They didn't need anyone but thought that Bob, the owner of Lakewood Camera, might.

I called Bob, and he asked me to come in to talk the next day. After a very informal interview, Bob said, "Let's give it a try for a few days and we'll see how you do."

Wearing a white shirt, black dress slacks, and skinny black necktie, I started the next morning.

Now, I need to digress to explain why I thanked Edwin Land.

When I was about 12 years old, my father invested in a Polaroid Land Camera for our family. I say invested because, if I remember correctly, the Polaroid camera cost about $150...a LOT of money in those days. It was, at that time, an amazing device, allowing you to take a black and white photograph and see it 60 seconds later.

The original Land Cameras were heavy, complicated, and not very easy to use. Loading the film could be confusing because there were two different rolls and they had to be loaded correctly so they came together, properly aligned, inside the camera after the photo was taken. Instinctively, I knew how to do this, like the way kids today instinctively know how to use a smartphone.

Lakewood Camera in 1965

My first day working at Lakewood Camera, a customer purchased a roll of Polaroid film. I rang up the sale and before leaving the store, he asked if anyone could help him load his camera.

I said, "Sure."

My boss, Bob, and the customer were surprised when I expertly loaded his camera in less than a minute.

"I guess you've got yourself a job," said Bob.

Thank you, Edwin Land.

Looking for Love (in All the Wrong Places)

No, I wasn't looking for love in all the wrong places. I was looking for love—or at least a girlfriend—but that had nothing to do with this situation. I had started working at Lakewood Camera just days earlier and felt sure that because of my failure to perform a simple task, I would lose my job. I couldn't find the store's shelf stretcher.

The store was in Lakewood Center, one of the earliest and largest shopping centers in the country. Stores were spread-out over the halfmile between Del Amo and Candlewood streets. The camera store where I worked was closer to the middle of the shopping center than toward either end.

Shortly after we opened for the day, Bob said that we were going to do some rearranging. He asked me to go to Buffum's department store on the north end of the shopping center and get our shelf stretcher back. Bob said he had lent it to the manager of the Men's department. Easy, I thought.

After the manager to finished with a customer, he politely told me that he had lent the device to the manager of the shoe department at JCPenny. Penny's, of course, was on the opposite end of the shopping center. No big deal. I walk fast.

The manager of the shoe department was on break when I got there, and I had to wait about 15 minutes for him to return. I was worried that Bob would be expecting me back by now. The shoe department manager was courteous when he explained that he had lent the shelf stretcher to the assistant manager at another store. I don't remember the name, but of course, the other store was at the opposite end of the shopping center, the same place I had been 15 minutes earlier.

I think that I went to five or six stores, each just about as far as possible from each other, trying to find that damn shelf stretcher. I was frustrated and anxious. Walking back to Lakewood Camera empty-handed, I worried that I'd be fired. When Bob saw the look on my face, he burst out laughing. I didn't understand, and was near tears when Bob said, "I guess you passed your initiation!"

To this day, I wonder where that damn shelf stretcher wound up?

Phoenix, Alaska?

You may be reading this and wonder if I'm claiming Phoenix is a town or city in Alaska that you have, somehow, never heard of. Or, more likely, you think I screwed up and substituted Alaska for Arizona. Neither is the case

Working at Lakewood Camera was a lot of fun. I got paid a dollar an hour to do something that I might have done for free—spend most of the day talking photography to customers and hanging out with tons of cool toys: cameras, projectors, tape recorders, and hi-fi systems.

My boss, Bob, owned the store and was only about 30 years old. Bob worked hard to make his business successful and expected his employees to work hard too.

The stuff that we sold was not something to fool around with. When we were not taking care of customers, we were supposed to be doing something useful - cleaning the glass countertops, dusting shelves, or straightening up. So, when I decided to play with a walkie-talkie one slow afternoon, I knew that I was doing something that could get me in trouble, but I couldn't resist.

Bob was in his office, and there were no customers in the store. Of all the cool stuff we had in the store, I was most fascinated by a pair of walkie-talkies. I think the pair sold for about $400 which would have been more than a month's pay for me. I quietly took one of the walkie-talkies off the shelf and went out to the sidewalk in front of the store. I pulled up the telescoping antenna, turned the unit on and tried to reach...anyone.

Holding down the talk button, I said, "Come in. Come in. Can anyone hear me?"

I think I repeated this at least a half-dozen times hoping that somebody, anybody would answer me. I was just about to give up when I heard a scratchy voice faintly reply "Hello. This is Artuk in Phoenix, Alaska. Come in, come in. I need help!"

"This is Lakewood California. This is Lakewood California!" I yelled into the device.

After a few seconds, I heard the faint scratchy voice again. "Hello, hello. This is Artuk in Phoenix, Alaska. I need help. Come in, come in!"

Now, I was in a jam. What started as me playing around with this walkie-talkie had turned into serious business. There was a guy in Alaska that needed help, which meant that I had to do something. But, what?

I only paused a moment thinking about the trouble I might get in, then ran back into the store to get help from my boss. There he was, sitting at his desk with the other walkie-talkie in his hand. I could tell he was mad, but I could also tell he was trying hard not to laugh. Handing me the walkie-talkie he had been using Bob said sternly, "Put these away and don't play with them again! Understand?"

I never touched those damn walkie-talkies again.

I Didn't Do It!

Once again, I did not follow my father's advice and, because of that, both my mom and dad thought it wasn't safe for me to ride my motor scooter.

Before I was able to buy a car, my parents bought me a well-used ISO motor scooter. You likely have never heard of an ISO motor scooter because the company, ISO Autoveicoli S.p.A of Italy went out of business years ago.

I finally had transportation! My walking everywhere days were over.

The only rule my dad tried to drill into my head was that I not let others ride my motor scooter. I didn't ask why he felt this was important, but to my detriment, I didn't follow this simple rule.

One Sunday after church, someone that I didn't know very well asked me if he could try out my ISO. Wanting to be a good guy, I said, "Sure."

He hopped on, started the bike, put it into gear, accelerated down the parking lot, and a few seconds later, crashed through thick shrubs breaking the left mirror off the bike and bloodying both of his arms and face. When my dad asked what happened, I took the blame for crashing my bike.

My best friend, George, asked if he could ride my motor scooter and of course, I said, "Yes."

George lasted several minutes before he laid it down on the asphalt tearing the skin off one of his legs and the paint off the side of my bike. Again, not wanting to admit that I had ignored my dad's rule, I took the blame for being clumsy.

It was only after another guy that I hardly knew crashed my motor scooter into a wall and bent the front fender against the tire that I figured out that my dad's rule was a good one to follow.

That was the last time I let anyone ride my scooter and I finally fessed-up to my dad what had happened.

"I didn't do it...I didn't crash my scooter once! I let others ride my ISO, and they crashed it."

My dad said he wasn't surprised because, after each accident, he noticed that while the bike was beat-up, I didn't have a scratch on me.

I only had my ISO motor scooter for about a year. There was something wrong with the carburetor, and my dad couldn't find the parts needed to fix it. Each week it seemed to run worse, and finally, it stopped running at all.

Once again, I was walking. Walking and trying to save money to buy a car.

It Was There This Morning

Do camera stores typically sell paint?

It was fun working at Lakewood Camera and probably the most enjoyable time was when Bob, Jerry, and I were working together. Jerry was about my age, or possibly a year older. The three of us worked a lot of hours together and often hung out after work.

The store was open every day except Sunday. On Monday, Thursday, and Friday, we were open late, until 9:00 p.m. Weekdays were usually very slow, and we'd often go an hour or more without a single customer. So, when someone did come in, we gave them our full attention whether they were there to buy something or not.

Late one morning an elderly lady came in, struggling to carry a gallon paint can. She asked what happened to the paint store that had been next door to the camera store.

Without missing a beat Bob said, "What do you mean? It's right there." He pointed at the music store that had taken the place of the paint store.

"It was there this morning," chimed in Jerry.

"I saw it when I came in," I added.

We all gave the poor lady the impression that the paint store had somehow changed into a music store within the past couple of hours. She stood there totally bewildered. Bob, Jerry, and I started laughing.

The paint store had, in fact, moved out of the shopping center more than a year earlier. We fessed up to the teasing, apologized profusely, and told her where the paint store was and how to get there.

Without moving a step and obviously still confused she asked, "Well, do you have another gallon of this paint?"

The Bank Deposit

Unlike many other countries, banking regulations in the U.S. are highly fragmented. The FDIC, Federal Reserve Board, and the Office of the Comptroller of the Currency all play a role in regulating banking. This story will not discuss such a mind-numbing subject, rather the lack of regulation over my actions in making the camera store's bank deposit.

A branch of Farmers and Merchants Bank was located at the intersection of Candlewood and Greywood, about a five-minute walk from the camera store where I worked. As I gained experience and the trust of my boss, I was given more and more responsibility. In addition to making sure a fresh cup of coffee, served how they liked it, was on the counter when one of our regular customers came in, I was entrusted with making the daily bank deposit.

Our business was mainly cash with some customers paying by check. Credit cards were very uncommon, and the store did not accept Diners Club or Carte Blanche, which I think were the only credit cards in use at that time. The daily deposit was typically less than a thousand dollars.

In order to help business customers keep their deposits safe, the bank gave us a sturdy brown leather bag with a handle and a lock. Once locked by the business, whoever was carrying the deposit to the bank could not open the bag. It could only be opened by a teller at the bank. Bob thought anyone seeing one of the leather bags would immediately recognize it and know the bag contained money. Not wanting our deposit to attract attention and be stolen, my boss came up with a unique plan.

To be less conspicuous, we put our cash, checks, and the deposit slip in one of our small brown Lakewood Camera paper bags. The assumption was that anyone looking would see a bag from the camera store and assume it was photographs of Aunt Sally or the grandkids. In other words, worthless, and not worth stealing.

One summer day, I was in a good mood and happy to get out of the store and walk to the bank. As I was walking, I was swinging the deposit bag. As I crossed the street to the bank, and the bag was at the apex of my swing, everything fell out! The wind was blowing, and the cash and checks blew into the busy intersection. Cars were zooming by, and if I was to have any chance of getting our cash and checks back, I had to jump into the street and stop traffic...which I did.

While horns blared, I was down on my hands and knees with one hand up trying to hold back traffic while trying to pick up the fives, 10s, 20s, and checks with my other hand. Some drivers must not have realized I had the authority to stop traffic, so they drove through the intersection running over checks and cash, and nearly running over me.

It seemed much longer at the time, but it probably took me less than five minutes to recover all the cash, all the checks, and even the deposit slip. Going into the bank, I guess I was quite a sight. I had torn my pants, and my knees were bleeding. My shirt was untucked (and in those days shirts were not untucked!), and my hands were filthy. Having stuffed the checks and cash back into the bag, I gave the contents to a teller.

"What happened to these checks? What happened to this cash? What happened to you?" were three rapid-fire questions from the young female teller

I explained what had happened and she laughed as she replied, "So, that's what all of the honking and commotion outside was about!"

Amazingly, I had recovered all the deposit. If I had not, I would probably have had to make up any shortfall from my meager earnings. The scabs on my knees took a week or so to heal, and my only real loss was the $20 bucks (two days' work) to buy a new pair of dress pants. However, I learned an important banking lesson that day. Be very careful with your boss's money.

When I got back to the store, my boss asked unsympathetically, "What took you so long?"

Then, seeing my torn pants and disheveled appearance he added, "And what the hell happened to you?"

I handed Bob the deposit receipt and without further explanation said, "I need to go clean up."

Goliath

You may not believe this, but my first car was a Goliath...honest. Friends that are car enthusiasts have insisted that there was no such car, but they are wrong. I owned and drove a Goliath.

Being 17 and not having a car was a bummer! I typically walked but also begged rides from my friends. Not having a car made it especially challenging to have a girlfriend. I wanted a car and the freedom that came with owning a car. My problem was money. I had only been able to save $200. Today you can drop that on a meal, but in 1963, $200 was more than I earned in a month.

Once I had saved up $200...and that took me all summer...I bugged my dad until he took me car shopping. We only spent a few minutes at each car lot because when my dad explained how much I had to spend the reply was, "We don't have anything that cheap."

Finally, at a car lot in nearby Bellflower aptly named Auto Liquidators, the salesman showed us a small black foreign car that, in the dark, looked pretty good and...cost $200.

We walked around the car and couldn't see any major body damage. The salesman started up the engine and allowed my dad to drive it around the block. It ran, so I figured that was good enough. I bought it. It was not until the next day that I realized that I had purchased a car named Goliath!

Goliath was a car manufactured in Germany by Borgward Lloyd Werks in Bavaria, the home of BMW! Mine was a four-cylinder, four -stroke front-wheel drive model 1100. Wikipedia claims that it was manufactured and branded Goliath for only two years, 1957 and 1958. Mine was a '57.

In the '60s all gas stations were full service. When you pulled into a gas station, one or more attendants rushed to assist. One would ask how much gas you wanted, and the other would open the hood to check the oil and fluids. Without exception, when the hood of my Goliath was popped open, the attendant was surprised.

As far as I know, this was the only front-wheel drive car on the streets of California at the time. The guy opening the hood would typically call others over to look at the German engineering marvel of my car's engine and transaxle, something they had never seen.

The name might lead you to think the Goliath was a large car. It was not. It was also not a fast car with a claimed top speed of 75 miles per hour, but I don't think I was ever able to get it above 60. The only vehicle that seemed to be slower than my Goliath was the humble Nash Metropolitan.

My Goliath was a two-door model with two bench seats. We got six of us in it at one time, but it was extremely crowded. With three in the front, I hardly had room to turn the steering wheel or shift gears. It had an AM radio (that didn't work), but that was about it for amenities. There was no heater and of course no air conditioning.

A couple of weeks after I bought it, I drove back to Auto Liquidators to pickup the tags. The salesman who sold me the car laughed out loud as he commented that he was surprised that it was still running.

My Goliath was unique. As far as I have been able to tell, only about 20 were sold as new cars in California. Replacement parts were less than scarce, there just weren't any available. After a few months driving, the column-mounted shift linkage broke, making my car undrivable. My dad solved the problem by replacing the part of the linkage that switched between first and second gear and third and fourth gear with a well-greased straightened metal clothes hanger. It worked.

The part that the clothes hanger replaced was encased in a metal shaft and pushed or pulled a lever on the transmission. A newly replaced, well-greased clothes hanger would last about a month. I became skilled at replacing this vital part and always carried three or four straightened clothes hangers in the trunk, along with the tools necessary for a quick on-the-road exchange.

A much bigger problem developed that could we could not fix. The starter motor died. We searched for a replacement by calling auto parts stores all around Southern California. (It would be more than 30 years before there was such a thing as a web search! If you needed to find something you looked up potential stores in the yellow pages of the phone book and called them, one at a time.) We couldn't find a replacement. The solution was to push-start my car, and I got very good at doing that.

When you know that you will have to push-start your car, you become very careful about where you park. You never, ever park where anyone can block you in. I always looked for a parking spot with even the slightest slope and faced the car in that direction. Fortunately, if I got my Goliath moving forward at all, I could jump in, push in the clutch, put the car into first gear, pop the clutch and it would start...most of the time.

My friends and I put many miles on my Goliath. I drove it for about two years before I was able to save $600 and purchase a bright red '56 Volkswagen Bug, which didn't need to be pushed to get it started. I gave the Goliath to my best friend George. A few weeks later, my mom and dad saw George pushing the Goliath to jump-start it and laughed.

I have never seen another Goliath. If I still owned it today, it would be one of the rarest of automobiles! And, people would believe me when I told them that I drove a Goliath.

Doing Donuts in a Parking Lot

No, I didn't do "donuts" in the parking lot in my Goliath. It would not go fast enough for the tires to squeal and leave rubber.

My mom did not learn to drive until older than most. The main reason was that we only had one car and my dad drove that. We finally got her a used car so that she did not have to depend upon others for rides when my dad was at work.

My dad was my mom's primary driving instructor, but one Sunday afternoon, she asked me to take her out driving. She wanted to practice backing up, so we went to Lakewood Shopping Center, which had a huge parking lot. In the mid-60s, none of the stores were open on Sunday, so the parking lot was empty.

Mom wanted to practice a Y turn, which was a maneuver required to pass the behind-the-wheel drivers test. As I suggested, she put her right arm on the top of the bench seat, looked over her right shoulder, and steered with her left hand. Backing-up while turning, she pushed down on the accelerator a little too hard. We lurched backward, and this caught her off guard. Instead of taking her foot off the accelerator and applying the brakes, she hit the gas, and we started going backward faster and faster in a circle with the tires squealing. We were going so fast that I was pinned against the passenger door.

There were no cars or obstructions around us, so I wasn't worried as Mom did a few donuts in reverse. She was crying, but I was laughing.

"Mom, just take your foot off the gas," I said several times.

It took her a revolution or two with tires screeching for her to understand what she needed to do. We finally came to a stop with no harm done! We changed places, and I drove home. I promised not to tell anyone what had happened, until now.

After more weeks of practice, my mom finally gained enough confidence to schedule her behind-the-wheel driver's test. I took her to the DMV office in nearby Bellflower. I was proud of my mom and confident that she would pass as she drove off with the inspector in the passenger seat.

It seemed like my mom's driving test was taking longer than expected. Several drivers that had left after her to take their test had already returned. I feared that she was not doing well and was having to repeat some maneuvers, possibly the dreaded Y turn.

Sitting on the curb looking down the street, I saw the inspector walking back to the DMV office.

"Your mom is about five blocks down and to the right. She didn't pass her test and is sitting in her car, crying. She needs a lot more practice. You need to go and get her," he said.

It took a couple of tries, but my mom finally passed her behind-the-wheel test and got her driver's license! I am proud to say that she was an excellent driver and never had an accident or even received a traffic citation. And, we all got a good laugh when we convinced her that she needed to go to the gas station and ask to have the air changed on her tires.

It Was a Mad Mad Mad Mad World

I will never forget the day, November 22, 1963, the day President John F. Kennedy was shot and killed in Dallas, Texas.

I was at home getting ready to go to class at Cerritos College when I heard the news. Even though there was no social media or cell phones, by the time I got to school, everyone knew of the tragedy, but none of us knew what we were supposed to do. The school had not officially canceled classes, yet none of my instructors had shown up. Teachers and students milled around the campus in a daze.

We learned that the college had canceled our football game that evening. My best friend, Bob, and I had planned on going to the game. Now, I wondered what we would do?

Thinking back on that day, it seems irreverent that we did what we did.

"It's a Mad Mad Mad Mad World" was playing at the Cinerama Dome in Hollywood. Showings had been sold out since the movie opened a few weeks earlier. Bob and I took a chance and drove up to Hollywood thinking some might not show up and we could get tickets.

We did.

The show was nearly half-empty, and for 3 ½ hours, we were engrossed in the film and forgot about the profound sadness of the day our President was assassinated.

My Girlfriend Would Have Been Impressed

None of my friends had a house cleaner when they were 17, but I did. None of my friends had more than one job when they were 17, but I had three!

Money motivated me to work. For about six months, I had three part-time jobs. I worked 10 hours a week for Cerritos College cleaning the photo lab. My job at Memorial Hospital doing baby photos paid for 25 hours, but it never took me that long. A typical week at Lakewood Camera was 25 to 30 hours. These three jobs all paid minimum wage, which at the time, was $1.00 per hour. Oh, and I was taking a few classes at Cerritos College too.

Working three jobs and going to school, I felt I did not have the time to properly clean my small studio apartment. A neighbor of my mom and dads was doing house cleaning and looking for more work. If I remember correctly, she spent about four hours a week cleaning my apartment for $1.50 an hour.

Because of her cleaning and the fact that I was hardly ever there, my apartment was always spotless! I longed for a girlfriend and imagined that if I had one, she would be very impressed by my clean apartment!

The Summer of '64

By the summer of 1964, I had quit my other jobs and was working full time at Lakewood Camera. Working nearly 60 hours a week, my life revolved around the store. One of the significant events in the summer of '64 was the World's Fair in New York City. I didn't go to the fair, so I am not writing about that, rather an ongoing prank that finally ended when my boss went to the World's Fair.

This story centers around a red or blue hand towel. Thinking about how the color of the towel might affect the story, I realize that the color really doesn't matter. What matters is the effect that a 14 x 30 piece of cloth had on the lives of Bob, Jerry, and me in the summer of '64.

The camera store faced Hazelbrook Street and had parking right in front. As employees, we were supposed to leave the first dozen or so closest spaces for customers, so we parked a little way out. Typically, Bob, Jerry, and I parked our cars next to each other for no other reason than we took the first three spaces not reserved for customers.

During summer months, we often left our windows rolled down so that our cars were not as hot as ovens when we got into them. One day, when I left to go home for lunch, I found a crumpled-up blue hand towel lying on the front seat of my car. There was nothing special about this towel. It was just a plain blue hand towel. For no other reason than both of our windows were down, I picked up the towel and tossed it into Bob's car parked next to mine. That was it. I drove home for lunch and did not think anything about it.

A few days later when I was leaving for lunch, I found the blue towel on my seat again. Hmm? This time I was parked next to Jerry, so I tossed the towel into his car and left for lunch. That evening, the three of us closed the store for the day and headed out to our vehicles. When I got into mine, the blue towel was there...again. Quickly I picked it up, threw it into Bob's car, started my car and while I was backing out, the towel came flying back into my car. At this point getting rid of the blue towel seemed to become the thing to do.

The next day, I said I was going to lunch at the drugstore. (At that time, the Thrifty drugstore in Lakewood Center had a counter that served food.) I had a quick burger then snuck around into the parking lot, got the blue towel from my car, and intended to put into either Bob's or Jerry's car. Dang it! Both had the windows rolled up, and both were locked.

The day after was hot, so when I went to drive home for lunch, Bob's window was down. I tossed the towel into his car and drove home. Finishing lunch at home and getting into my car, I found the dreaded blue rag on my front seat! This was getting serious.

A day or so later. Bob said he was going to the Elks club for lunch. A short while after he drove off, I left Jerry alone to mind the store (we were not supposed to do this) and drove to the Long Beach Elks Lodge. I found Bob's car (it was easy, it was a bright yellow Mustang). The windows were up but his car was unlocked. He found the blue towel of course. Returning to the store, he balled it up and threw it at me!

The towel went back and forth every day or two. It became our preoccupation to find a way to get the blue rag into each other's car. I think more effort went into getting rid of that damn piece of cloth than running the store! It was our obsession.

Weeks went by with the blue towel changing hands almost daily. We knew that Bob would be leaving for New York to see the 1964 World's Fair because he talked about it every day. He was excited. Bob left information about his flights and the hotel where he would be staying.

In 1964 there were no delivery services like UPS or FedEx, and Priority Mail would not start for another seven years. If you wanted to ship a small package, you sent it by Parcel Post.

Allow me a true and interesting digression. A year after Parcel Post started in 1913, some very thrifty parents pasted 53 cents of postage onto their four-year-old daughter's coat and mailed her, using Parcel Post, to her grandparents who lived 70 miles away! Shortly after, Postal Regulations were changed to prohibit mailing live human beings! Charlotte May Pierstorff holds the honor of being the only person ever mailed.

About a week before Bob left, Jerry and I pooled our hard-earned cash, secretly packed up the blue towel, and spent $8.00 to mail it to his hotel in New York. We addressed the package to Head Bellman with a note asking him to put the enclosed towel in Bob's room when he arrived. We included a $5.00 bill as a big tip.

We never knew if that towel ever made it to New York and found its way into Bob's room but, we never saw it again. I think our plan must have worked because Bob never mentioned or asked about that damn blue towel when he got back.

Of Course, We Fix Lamps

The camera store that I worked at was open until 9:00 p.m. Monday, Thursday, and Friday evenings. Monday evenings were typically very slow. We'd often be lucky if a couple of customers came in. When no customers were in the store, Jerry and I were expected to clean, clean, and then clean some more.

One Monday evening, an elderly lady walked in struggling to carry a very large brass table lamp, complete with a lampshade. Seeing her struggle, I went around to the front of the showcase and helped her set her lamp on the counter as Bob and Jerry, looked on.

She timidly asked, "You repair lamps, don't you?"

"Of course, we do," yells my boss from across the store. "Come back in an hour, and we should have it fixed as good as new."

I shouldn't have been surprised by this, but I was.

There is not much that can go wrong with a table lamp. The bulb can burn out, the switch can malfunction, or one of the wires can come off the switch terminal. After the elderly lady left, it took us about five minutes to remove lampshade, the light bulb, take the switch housing apart and find that one of the wires had come off the switch terminal. The stripped portion of the copper wire had not been captured under the screw properly, and it was loose. The fix took seconds, and within a few minutes, we had the lamp reassembled and working perfectly.

About an hour later the lady came back, and as she walked into the store, she looked around. "This doesn't look like the lamp store," she said. "What kind of a store is this?"

"This is a camera store," said Bob. "But we fix lamps too."

The lady seemed confused, but her lamp was sitting on the counter, and we showed her that it worked. She thanked us and asked how much she owed us.

"We don't charge for fixing lamps," Bob said, and I helped her out to her car with her lamp.

After she left, we began to worry that she would come back with more lamps or even worse tell her friends, "That camera store in Lakewood Center fixes lamps for free."

As long as I worked at the camera store, that was the one, and only time someone came in to have their lamp fixed!

A Hundred Dollar Bet!

Howard Hughes had not yet become the world's first billionaire at the time of this story! And, in 1968, $100 was worth a whole lot more than it is today.

My boss, Bob, and his wife, Joann, liked to go to Vegas and they both seemed to like me to go with them. One Friday evening we flew to Vegas from Los Angeles on Western Airlines (The Only Way to Fly – at least that was their motto). We typically stayed at The Sands (torn down to make way for The Venetian), which was, at the time, THE place to be in Vegas. And, while The Sands was THE place to be, Circus Circus had recently opened to tremendous fanfare, and Bob wanted to see what all the buzz was about.

In the late '60s and early '70s, Circus Circus was unique. It was the only casino that catered to families with children. A level above the casino floor had games and amusements for kids. From the family area and the casino floor, you could watch nearly continuous circus acts above. It was pretty cool, except for the thick cigarette smoke that engulfed the whole building. Circus Circus had a restaurant above the casino that offered a great view of the circus acts. It was a high-end restaurant with tuxedoed waiters. I could not afford to eat there, but my boss could.

Bob must have tipped the maître d' because we were seated at a booth in the center of the restaurant with a great view of the circus acts. It was a real treat to be told, "Order anything you want."

We all ordered prime rib, and that's where this story begins.

When our meals were delivered, Joann asked for horseradish.

"Of course," our waiter replied and returned in a minute or so with what I would have accepted as horseradish.

"I'm sorry, I don't want horseradish sauce, I want fresh horseradish," said Joann.

"Raw horseradish is too hot," said Bob. "Just use what you have."

Joann was not someone who liked being told what to do. "I want fresh horseradish."

Bob and Joann argued, and each exchange got a little louder. Soon they were almost shouting. I was embarrassed and was looking back and forth at the two of them as if I were watching a tennis match. After several minutes of arguing our waiter brought Joann a small bowl of fresh horseradish.

"You made such a fuss about that, and I'll bet you are not even going to use enough to taste the difference," said Bob.

"How much will you bet?" Joann chided.

"I'll bet you $100 that you can't eat a teaspoon," challenged Bob.

Joann picked up a teaspoon, scooped up a heaping helping of horseradish and... ate it. I could see her eyes starting to water, but she resisted the urge to cool the inferno in her mouth with water.

"Pay up," she demanded in a gravelly voice.

We were unaware of it, but everyone seated around us had been witnessing the horseradish argument, and all joined in demanding Bob to pay up! Not wanting to look like a cheapskate, Bob pulled out a $100 bill and put it into Joann's waiting palm. The cheering from those around us made us all laugh, and the built-up tension between Bob and Joann was gone!

We're Going the Wrong Way

One of my very favorite movies is "Planes, Trains and Automobiles" starring Steve Martin and John Candy. There is a scene in the film where Martin and Candy are driving the wrong way on a divided highway. A couple in a car on the opposite side of the road are, of course, going in the same direction, yelling and trying to tell Candy and Martin that they are going the wrong way. John Candy laughs and says to Steve Martin, "They must be drunk because they don't know where we are going!"

One of my closest friends in high school got his private pilot's license right after he turned 16 years old. Wow! While other kids were starting to drive, Bob was flying an airplane. I thought that was awesome.

Bob flew out of Long Beach airport and took me up several times in one of his flight school Cessna 150 airplanes. The 150 was a high-wing two-seater with minimal instrumentation. It was also very small. Both Bob and I were skinny, yet we rubbed shoulders sitting in the cramped cockpit. The first few times Bob took me up, we flew around Long Beach Harbor, over our houses, and over our high school.

Let me explain a little more about Bob before I get to the story. Bob was a year behind me in school. His family lived in Lakewood and must have been better off than ours. Not only was Bob able to afford flying lessons, but his parents also bought him a fairly new Vauxhall sedan, which was a much nicer car than any of our friends had.

I am not sure how we wound up to be such good friends, but we did all kinds of crazy things together. One hot summer evening, we were sitting around doing nothing and decided that we wanted to go swimming. The beach was only about 6 or 7 miles away, but we drove 300 miles to Lake Havasu on the Colorado River. We swam for 10 or 15 minutes and then drove 300 miles back home. When our friends went to warm, sunny Palm Springs for Easter break, we camped in the snow at the base of Mount Whitney. We had fun doing crazy stuff.

Bob was smart and a much better student than I was, getting straight A's compared to my C's. I believe he was Valedictorian of his class and had a scholarship locked up even before his senior year.

One Sunday afternoon, Bob called to see if I wanted to go flying with him. Sure, I was always game. He picked me up, and we drove to Eagle Aviation at Long Beach airport. Bob filled out the paperwork to rent an airplane, but when he went to get the keys to the aircraft, he learned that the weather conditions were "special VFR." VFR means visual flight rules—that you can see where you are going, and you can see the ground. Special VFR allows a pilot to fly in conditions that are not as good as VFR. I am not sure of precisely what the rule requires, but Bob told me we had to stay out of clouds.

I helped Bob preflight the small two-seat airplane, and a few minutes later we took off from runway 25-Right and headed...into clouds. We were only in the clouds for a few minutes and came out the other side. Bob banked the plane as we climbed and headed toward the mountains. Thinking back on that day, this was not a smart thing to do.

As we got closer to 10,000-foot Mt Baldy, the airplane caught an updraft, and we began climbing rapidly. I watched the altimeter hand wind around, indicating our ever-increasing altitude above sea level. We soon topped 12,000 feet and were still climbing. As we were climbing, Bob was making a continuous corkscrew-like turn. There were huge clouds all around us, but we were in clear air.

Finally, at just over 15,000 feet, Bob yelled over the din of the engine, "There's not enough oxygen up here for us. We need to get down." Which sounded like an excellent idea to me.

Getting back to Long Beach airport should have been a snap. Bob dialed in the frequency for the VOR—a type of navigating system that uses a series of radio beacons—and said if he kept the needle centered, we'd be heading directly back to Long Beach.

Hmm, I thought. We were heading away from the sun, which was low in the sky as we gradually descended. I didn't bring this up at first, but after about 10 minutes we flew into very thick clouds.

Here we were, flying around mountains that topped 10,000 feet in thick clouds with no visibility and, in my mind, heading away from Long Beach airport.

I finally spoke up and said to Bob, "We're going the wrong way."

"How can you say that," Bob asked.

"Before we got into these clouds, we were flying away from the sun, which means we were heading east."

Bob, being a pretty smart guy, only thought for a few seconds before he realized that he had set the navigational compass to take us away from the VOR instead of toward the VOR and our desired destination...Long Beach Airport.

Bob changed the setting to take us toward Long Beach, and we made a wide turn, still descending. As each minute passed, it got darker and darker because the sun had set, and we were flying in thick clouds.

I do not believe Bob had much, if any, training to fly in IFR (Instrument Flight Rules) conditions—meaning flying using only instruments. Despite this, and even though visibility was zero, he kept the plane level and our decent controlled and gradual… as compared to crashing!

We flew along for 15 or 20 minutes gradually dropping to about 4,000 feet. We finally broke through the clouds and could see lights on the ground. We both recognized that we were above Corona and somewhat lower than 5,700-foot Santiago Peak off to our left. Another 20 minutes or so and we landed in light rain, in the dark, at Long Beach airport. We were very fortunate to have made it back safely.

That flight scared the crap out of me, and I have not flown in a private aircraft since.

An Afternoon Gone Bad

It was a late, sweltering summer afternoon. I was sitting at my desk alone in the office when I was startled by someone pounding violently on the door. Before I even said come in, the door flew open and one of the largest and nastiest-looking men I had ever encountered barged in. He was holding a baseball bat in his right hand, waving it at me, totally enraged!

"You know who I am?" he barked.

"Who the hell are you and what the hell are you doing here?"

I had a '38 in my desk drawer but could not remember whether or not it was loaded. Even if it were loaded, I was not sure that I knew how to use it. But, I thought, if I pulled it out and laid it on my desk, it might give me an advantage for whatever was going to happen next.

"You're the asshole that's representing my whore of a wife. Now you know why I'm here?" he snarled. "She's not gettin' a cent of my money! You hear me, asshole? Not a cent! If she does, you're the one who's gonna pay, and you're gonna pay with your life!"

Slowly, I opened my desk drawer, reached in and just as I grasped the handle of my '38, he –

Oops, wrong story. What the heck is going on? I guess I was daydreaming.

I Thought I Was Going to Maine!

One of the most intense experiences of my life was the 2 ½ years I spent in Japan as a Mormon missionary.

At this point, I need to digress to explain how I wound up becoming a Mormon and going on a mission to Japan.

One of the girls that I was interested in during my sophomore year in high school was Marjorie. She was a junior, a year ahead of me, but was very friendly and seemed to like hanging out with me. She was a Mormon, and her church had a lot of fun things for kids our age. Becoming friends with her friends eventually led me to go to church with her on Sundays.

My Mormon friends had lots of parties, dances, beach trips, and barbecues. We had a lot of fun without alcohol or tobacco, which were taboo to good Mormons. My two best non-Mormon friends, Bob and Tom, didn't drink or smoke and, in those days, at least at Mayfair High School, using drugs was rare. I have since joked that the class of '63 was the last "good" class at Mayfair.

In my junior year, something terrible happened. Marjorie's family moved from Lakewood to Upland, about 45 miles away. Forty-five miles does not seem that far today, but in 1962 there were no 405, 605, 55, 57, 60, or 91 freeways. Most of the drive to Upland was on secluded, and very dark at night, Brea Canyon Road. With no traffic on the two lane, winding road, the trip took more than an hour. I think the distance and the fact that I was working as a bowling scorekeeper most evenings doomed our relationship. That fact that she met a guy she liked at Upland High School may have also played a role.

Be that as it may (I think this is the very first time that I have ever in my life used that phrase), I continued to be a good Mormon. I went to church every Sunday. Mormon young men are expected to go on a mission shortly after they turn 19 years old. I was no exception.

In the spring of '65, I received a letter from the church telling me that I was chosen to go to the Northern Far East Mission. I figured that I was going to Maine. Good! Maine was on the opposite side of the country, but I was relieved. I wouldn't have to worry about learning a foreign language, and the food wouldn't likely be a problem. A few weeks later, I was confused when a letter came giving me instructions to get a U.S. Passport and apply for a visa to Japan!

After a week of orientation in Salt Lake City, 14 of us left for Japan on June 29th, 1965. We stopped in San Francisco and Anchorage Alaska, arriving at Haneda airport in Tokyo

It wasn't a ticket to fly to Maine!

the next evening. When the aircraft stopped, I looked out the window on a foggy world. It must be cold, I thought, so I put on my suit coat and overcoat. Seeing me do that, the others in our group followed my example. We exited the plane, bundled up against the expected cold and into the steaming heat and humidity of Tokyo in the summer. The other passengers surely had a good laugh as we struggled to get our coats, jackets, and hats off as quickly as possible.

Our group stayed in the Mission Home in Tokyo for four or five days, and I was the last to leave. One of the mission home staff took me to catch a train to Takasaki, where I would be living for the next four months. I boarded the train at Ueno *Eki* (station) holding a slip of paper with Takasaki written in both romaji (English lettering) and kanji 高崎. The train was full, so I had to stand. At each stop, I looked out the window at the station sign and compared it to what I had in my hand. Finally, after a couple of hours, I recognized the name Takasaki and was able to get off the train with my luggage before the doors closed.

There was no one to meet me!

I found my way outside the station and had no idea where to go or what to do. I was standing in the middle of the street looking around with my large suitcase and no idea what to do next. I couldn't read any of the signs, and I didn't think that I could ask for help because I had yet to learn to speak any Japanese.

I don't remember how long I stood there, but a teenage girl finally came up to me and bashfully asked, "Morumon missionary?"

Very relieved to hear recognizable English, I eagerly responded, "Yes!"

She hailed a taxi and took me to the house where the missionaries lived.

The house was a small, typical Japanese home that, at the time, did not have such niceties as a flushing toilet, as homes in rural Japan in 1965 were often not connected to a sewer system. While the *benjo* (toilet room) was very clean, it sat over a concrete pit that held what it was supposed to hold. The smell was not something that I will ever forget! It made me appreciate bathrooms back at home.

So, here I was in July of 1965, living in a relatively small Japanese city. Takasaki was, in many ways, a lot farther from my home in Lakewood than the 5,700 miles! But it was to be my home for the next four months, as the weather changed from hot and humid summer to a frigid winter.

Not knowing a single person, not speaking Japanese, not knowing what I would be doing, I wondered what I had gotten myself into! I was a long way from home in California and even farther from Maine.

A Package of Napkins

You may remember the chapter, "A Bag of Potato Chips" from earlier. This is not a similar story because I wanted to do as I was asked, and I didn't mutilate the napkins that I had bought on the way home from the store.

To set the scene so that you might understand my embarrassment, I had only been in Japan a few weeks and could only speak about 20 words of Japanese. By speak, I mean that I had memorized a few common phrases. "Watakushi wa Mancini Choro Desu. Yoroshiku onegaishimasu." (Translation: I am Elder Mancini. Please be kind to me.) I understood NO Japanese when it was spoken to me. The six of us that lived together were about to have dinner. Dinner generally consisted of pork or fish along with a generous serving of gohan...white rice.

Divergence warning.

I must explain one of the big differences between living in the U.S. and living in Japan—at least in 1965. Before living in Japan, I had eaten plain, white rice precisely zero times! This was not because I did not like rice, rather it was never once offered to me. Not only had I not eaten rice, I had never even seen another person eat rice! I would not have known what it was unless someone said, "Hey, that's rice."

Shortly after arriving in Japan I started eating rice. By this, I mean I had rice at every meal...breakfast, lunch, and dinner. Japanese people would ask how many times a day I had rice in America and could not believe it when I said zero. Rice is such an essential part of the Japanese diet that the word for rice in Japanese, *gohan*, is used as the same word for food.

I also had to learn that you don't mess with rice in Japan. One of the first times I had dinner in Japan I attempted to get some ketchup to put on my plain white rice. Yikes...this seemed to be as serious a blunder as stabbing someone in the heart with chopsticks. (*Ohashi*...chopsticks...are also something that you did not fool around with in Japan). Rice was to be eaten as presented, plain. No ketchup, salt, pepper, or anything!

We were getting ready to have dinner when someone realized we were out of napkins. I think the sentiment was, send the new guy to the store, and I was the new guy. This was unusual because we never went out alone. We always went two-by-two, typically with our assigned companion (more about this later). I guess because the small shop was only about 100 yards away, I was trusted to run this errand on my own.

The little shop seemed to carry everything a family might need. Because I couldn't ask for what I was looking for, I tried on my own to find a package of dinner napkins. I probably spent 5 to 10 minutes looking at packages, none with any English writing, trying to find napkins. All this time, the *tenshu* (shopkeeper) eyed me wearily. I think he asked several times if he could help me, but that is only a guess because I had no idea what he was saying. Finally, I mouthed the word napkin, which he didn't understand as evidenced by him scrunching up his face and scratching his head.

Because the little shop seemed to sell just about everything, I was pretty sure there were napkins to be had, but I couldn't find them. Trying to be both helpful and respectful, the shopkeeper laid a pencil and piece of paper on the counter and pointed to it. I got the idea. Write down what it was that I was looking for. NAPKIN.

"Ahhhhh, ahhhhhh, choto mate kudasai." (I did not understand this at the time, but now, knowing some Japanese, I think this is what he probably said.) Translation: "Ahhhhh, ahhhhhh, wait just a moment, please."

In a few moments, the shopkeeper was wrapping my purchase carefully in colorful paper. OK, I need to digress again. Nearly, EVERY PURCHASE IN JAPAN IS CAREFULLY WRAPPED IN ATTRACTIVE PAPER. Subsequent business trips in the '90s and even when my wife and I visited in Japan in 2013, confirmed that anything you purchase has to be wrapped before you leave the store. This practice is so universal that I suspect that it may be a law. (Actually, it is just a custom, but customs in Japan seem to be as strictly adhered to as if they were a law!) The wrapping is not fancy like gift wrap, but every purchase is carefully and attractively wrapped.

So, back to the story. After the shopkeeper wrapped the package of napkins, it was time to pay. But I had no idea how much to pay. Taking the Japanese bills and coins from my pocket and placing them on the counter the shopkeeper carefully counted out some amount of Yen (the Japanese currency), and I left the store very pleased with myself.

When the package was opened, there was a great deal of laughter. I had purchased a box of *Josei-yo napukin*...feminine napkins! Not only was there a good laugh and lots of ribbing at dinner that night, but the story of my mistake soon spread to missionaries in other parts of Japan, and I became known as the guy who doesn't know what feminine napkins are!

The Amazing Race

"The Amazing Race" is, and has been for years, my very favorite TV show. This story has very little to do with that show, except that contestants on "The Amazing Race" must always stick close to each other, like my missionary experience.

"The Amazing Race" participants are teams of two people. They are often good friends, parents and children, or dating couples. Unless instructed explicitly during the race, team members must always stay within 20 feet of each other. I wonder if they got this from the rules that Mormon missionaries must follow?

Mormon missionaries are assigned companions and are required to always be near or within sight of their designated companion. One of the most significant adjustments that I had to make as a new missionary was staying near my assigned companion and not having any time alone! That was difficult for me, and I often found myself longing to wander off alone...but I didn't.

When I left the mission home in Tokyo and headed to my first posting in Takasaki, one of the few things I knew was who would be my assigned companion. And, within a few days of working together, I realized that I didn't like him very much. It was not that there was anything wrong with him; we just didn't get along very well. I was his last companion as his mission would end in four months. He would be going home, and probably thought that taking care of a "green bean" (what new missionaries were called) was a pain-in-the-ass. I would be assigned a new companion when he left.

While I did not care for my first companion, I depended upon him. He spoke Japanese, and I did not. He knew his way around the city, and I did not. He knew how to use the *Kōshū yokujō* (public bath) properly, and I did not. I needed my first companion even though he was someone who I didn't like very much.

During the 2 ½ years that I was a missionary, I had nine different companions. Regardless of how much we liked each other…or not, we always found a way to live and work well together. It was an excellent lesson for a 20-year-old.

Throughout my career, I often found myself in a similar position. I may not have liked a boss or subordinate, but my experience with my missionary companions helped me work successfully with them. Looking back on my career, I think I won my own very amazing race.

Climate Change

By November, it was cold in Takasaki, Japan. It wasn't climate change, rather the start of winter!

I don't think we had a working heater in the missionary quarters, so we depended upon our electric blankets to keep us warm throughout the night. The six of us slept in three bunk beds in the same small room. I was on one of the top bunks, and the controller for my electric blanket often slipped down, which meant that I couldn't reach it to adjust it during the night. While lying in my bunk shivering one night, I had an idea!

The next afternoon there was a period when I was the only one in our room. I went over to one of the other bunk beds and stretched the controller from the electric blanket on the top bunk down to the bottom bunk and the controller for the bottom bunk up to the top bunk. If anyone looked carefully, they would see the wires to the controllers were crossed, but no one noticed.

Sometime in the middle of the night, the guy who was in one of the other bunks tried to adjust the temperature of his electric blanket. With the wires crossed, this changed the temperature of whoever was in the other bed. To compensate for the temperature change, the guy in the other bed adjusted what he thought was the temperature of his electric blanket. This must have happened several times before we were all woken up by the guy on the top bunk yelling that he thought his electric blanket had shorted out because it was so hot!

I believe there were some inappropriate (e.g., unmissionary-like) words used as his cover and blanket went flying off his bunk! Without ever really waking up, the guy on the bottom bunk grabbed the cover that had been thrown off the top bunk and added it to his chilly bed.

I never fessed up to my part of what went on that cold October night, but the bunkmates figured out that the wires to their controllers were crossed the next day. I have always wanted to repeat that prank but haven't had the opportunity...yet.

Deja Vu

dé·jà vu – noun – a feeling of having already experienced the present situation.

Being Mormon missionaries, the options to have fun were limited, very limited! But being 20 years old and living with five other 20-year-old guys meant that we were always trying to find ways to have fun.

Just before I received a transfer from Takasaki to Futenma Okinawa, it was one of the other missionary's birthday. The other five of us decided to have some fun at his expense.

Part of a Mormon missionary's life is to wake up promptly at 6:00 every morning. It was dark at 6:00 a.m. in Takasaki in late October. This fact provided us the opportunity to pull off a pretty good prank.

We had wrapped a few small presents, had a birthday card, and a small cake. My alarm went off at 3:00 a.m., and I quietly woke the other guys, except for Richard. We gathered around Richard's bottom bunk and woke him singing happy birthday very loudly with candles lit on the small cake.

Being woken in the middle of the night, it took the birthday boy a few minutes to figure out what was happening.

"Hey, it's your birthday. Make a wish and blow out your candles," one of the other guys said.

There was a lot of laughter and joking around as we gave Richard his birthday card and small presents. It took about 10 minutes to get through the present opening and joking about the birthday card, and THEN, we told Richard, "Look at your clock."

Seeing it was about 3:15 a.m., Richard asked, "Awe geese. Are we supposed to stay up?"

"NO," the rest of us answered in unison.

After making sure that Richard had fallen back to sleep, I put new candles in the cake, rewrapped the presents, put the birthday card in a new envelope, and sealed it. I woke up at about a quarter to six and woke the other guys. At 6:00 a.m., the five of us gathered around the sleeping missionary's bunk and repeated what we had done a few hours earlier, waking Richard to our singing happy birthday with candles lit on the small cake.

Richard opened his eyes and looked frightened. As we continued singing Happy Birthday, he cheered up and started smiling. When he opened his birthday card, a dark look came over his face.

"I swear I knew what this card said before I opened it," muttered Richard.

Opening the first present, a book, Richard became quiet and said, "I knew what book this was before I unwrapped it."

We all laughed and continued to laugh as Richard, looking sullen, opened his other presents.

"What's wrong?" we asked. "Don't you like your presents?"

"It's just that I swear that I knew what my presents were and exactly what was going to happen next."

"Déjà vu," one of the others replied.

"I guess, but this is the creepiest feeling that I have ever had," groaned Richard.

I left Takasaki a week or so later for Okinawa, and as far as I know, no one told Richard of our prank.

A Toothache

How entertaining can a chapter about a toothache be? You can decide after reading it.

It was mid-November when I got the call to leave Takasaki, take the train to Tokyo, and fly to Okinawa. The best part of the transfer was that for the first time in over four months, I was alone for a whole day as I traveled! I went from very cold and overcast Takasaki to hot and sunny Okinawa.

The Mormon branch in Futenma was tiny compared to Takasaki, having only a handful of members. It was located directly across a road from the end of the runway at MCAS (Marine Corps Air Station) Futenma. This was during the Vietnam War, and noise from aircraft landing and taking off was a 24/7 constant. We lived in an old cinderblock military building with a corrugated metal roof. The missionary quarters were a single room with a small table, four chairs, and two sets of bunk beds. A compact kitchen and a larger room took up the rest of the building and were used for church services.

Not long after arriving in Okinawa, I started experiencing a painful tooth. Day by day, my toothache became more and more severe. Finally, it was so painful that I couldn't eat or function and needed to do something about it. But I had no idea what to do. I didn't know of a dentist or even how to find a dentist.

The missionary in charge of the branch finally called the mission home in Tokyo. A few hours later, he received a call back with an address and instructions to take me to a dentist in nearby Ginowan City.

The dentist office was not what I expected. It appeared that the middle-aged dentist practiced in the front room of his home. The small office was immaculate, and I remember the dental chair had a white lacy doily so that the patient's hair would not touch the back of the dentist chair.

The dentist did not seem to speak any English. But, not speaking English did not seem to be a problem as he immediately understood by my moaning and pointing to the back of my mouth that I needed his immediate attention.

It only took a few moments for the *oisha san* (dentist) to hit the problem tooth with an instrument, which caused me to nearly jump out of his chair.

"Ahhhh, ahhhh, ahhhh," seemed to indicate that he understood what the problem was. He gave me a shot of Novocain (at least I think it was a shot of Novocain) and a few minutes later pulled the badly infected wisdom tooth, which hurt like hell.

Really!

The dentist gave me a small, unmarked bottle of pills and holding up three fingers on one hand and a single finger on the other seemed to indicate that I needed to take three of the pills each day. I did not know what the pills were, but because they offered absolutely no pain relief, I think they might have been antibiotics.

The dentist left the room, and a few minutes later came back with a slip of paper written in Japanese. He bowed and presented the bill for his services. If I remember correctly, the amount was 1,000 yen which was equivalent to $2.80 U.S. dollars.

I don't know if it was the extraction, the infection, or both, but I was in severe pain. I stayed in my bunk for the next two long days. Finally, on the third day, the pain and swelling subsided, and I was able to eat for the first time in days.

Having a badly infected wisdom tooth pulled with only a shot of Novocain was so traumatic that I remember it well even after more than 50 years!

The World Had Changed

Race riots
Vietnam War protests
Martin Luther King Jr. shot
Robert F Kennedy shot
The Six Day War
Timothy Leary and LSD
Anti-War protests at the Democratic Convention
Hippies

I left Japan and the quiet and sheltered missionary life on December 29, 1967. I showed up at Lakewood Camera the next morning, hoping that I had my old job back, and I did. Thank you, Bob!

The world that I left in 1965 had changed dramatically during the 2 ½ years that I lived in Japan. Or had I changed?

I was shocked at the daily news about the Vietnam War. A war had been raging, and because as missionaries we had no access to TV, I knew very little about it while I was in Japan.

Race riots and civil rights protests seemed to be regular occurrences. Martin Luther King Jr. and Robert F Kennedy were both shot, and I thought to myself, Japan was so safe and so peaceful!

The Beatles had become popular in the 2 ½ years that I was gone, and something called psychedelic happened. There were a new group of kids called hippies. All that I knew about them was that they hung out in San Francisco, seemed to like flowers, and everyone seemed to think they were cool. What was I missing?

As a returned missionary, I was active at church but gradually became alienated. Perhaps because finding someone to date at church was not working out, and all the friends I used to hang out with at church were gone. I was also bothered that the church seemed to be politically very conservative and I was not. I was dismayed one Sunday when one of the leaders said that Mormons were expected to support Richard Nixon and the Republican Party. I resented this, and not long after, I stopped being a "good Mormon," which meant I eventually stopped going to church.

Gradually, the details of my life as a missionary in Japan faded and were replaced by my new life as a 23-year-old single guy enjoying life in Southern California. I grew long sideburns, wore bell-bottom pants, enjoyed work, and started to seriously look for a girlfriend.

'65 Mustang

Arriving back home from Japan I didn't have a car. I had sold my '56 VW Bug before I left, two and a half years earlier. Not having a car meant that I would walk to and from work at Lakewood Camera. That was OK with me because it was only 2 ½ miles and I walked more than that every day when I was in Japan.

My boss, Bob, decided his wife needed a larger car...a station wagon...and bought her one. She had been driving a 1965 dark green 289 Mustang, and their two kids were outgrowing the small back seat.

Bob gave me the Mustang!

When I say Bob gave me the Mustang, I mean he gave it to me to use. That was great because he continued to own it and pay the insurance which I could not afford. All I had to do was put gas in the car and keep it clean.

The 1968 Steve McQueen movie "Bullitt" featured a dark green Mustang that was a twin to the car Bob gave me. My Mustang had a three-speed manual transmission and the car in the movie, a four-speed. I think the movie car had a larger engine, but my friends were very impressed that I was driving the same car as in the hit movie.

At this time, Bob had purchased Mercury Camera in Long Beach, and I was the manager. Needing two people to staff the store, he hired a guy named Craig. He was about my age and a real photo enthusiast. We got along great and hung out after work. With neither of us having anything planned to do one weekend, we decided to drive to Vegas Saturday after work and come back Sunday morning, staying up all night.

We took the Mustang and made it to Vegas in record time, and without getting a speeding ticket. Craig had heard about a new casino, and we decided to check out The Landmark. At the time, it was the tallest building in Vegas and had a casino on the top floor. It stood across the street from the Convention Center until it was demolished in 1995 to make room for a parking lot.

Call it beginner's luck because when we left early Sunday morning, I had about $125 more than I had brought with me. I was a winner! We headed home about 10:00 a.m., exhausted, but still high from our allnight gambling.

About 15 miles out of town, the temperature gauge went all the way into the red, so we pulled over at a gas station in Sloan. The engine was hot, and it appeared that the radiator was empty. We let the engine cool down then filled the radiator with water figuring we had solved the problem. We were wrong.

Within another 10 miles, the engine was running very rough, and the temperature gauge shot up into the red again. Steam and smoke were pouring from the engine compartment as we limped along. We barely made it to Jean, a spot on the highway with no residents, and pulled into the first gas station we saw. Being a Sunday morning, only an attendant to pump gas was at the station, and he couldn't offer us any help except to call a tow truck.

It took almost an hour for the tow truck to show up. When it did, the tow truck driver had us start the Mustang's engine.

Hearing the noise coming from the engine, he yelled, "Shut it off! You've got a real problem. I think you've blown a head gasket or even thrown a rod."

Neither Craig nor I understood what this meant, but what it meant was we weren't going to be driving the Mustang home.

"A lot of the mechanics in Vegas will screw you because you're in from LA. I know a shop where they won't do that," the tow truck driver said.

We followed his advice, and he took us, with the Mustang in tow, to a repair shop 35 miles away at the North Las Vegas Airport.

Because it was Sunday, the shop was, of course, closed! Next to the repair shop and the airport was a small motel. Both Craig and I had been up since Saturday morning, and it was now late Sunday afternoon. We were both worn out. We were able to get a cheap room at the motel and crashed. When we woke up that evening, we were both starving, having not eaten anything since we had burgers on our way to Vegas.

The lady who ran the motel said that there was a restaurant that served good food and was reasonable a couple of miles up the road. She knew our car was not running and said we could use one of the airport's trucks. Going behind the motel, the only vehicle we could find was a pickup truck that had a huge FOLLOWME sign mounted behind the cab. It was the truck they used to guide planes around the airport! We drove it to the restaurant and back to the motel. Luckily, no aircraft followed us.

Having slept for a few hours and then eaten, Craig and I felt a lot better. I had been putting off calling Bob. I didn't want to tell him that the Mustang was broken-down in Vegas, but the time had come to do so.

"You know that you need to get back to open the store in the morning," was Bob's firm reminder.

"Of course," I replied, not knowing exactly how I was going to do that.

"Leave Craig there to handle the car," said Bob.

The first time I left Vegas as a winner, I wound up taking a Greyhound bus home. The bus dropped me off early Monday morning in Long Beach, a few blocks from the store. I opened on time, still wearing the clothes I had worn when I left on Saturday afternoon. I needed a shave and a shower but could only manage to wash up in the bathroom sink. It was a long day.

It cost $800 to have the Mustang's V8 engine rebuilt in 1969. Bob sent the money via Western Union, and Craig drove the car back to Long Beach four days later. He was wearing the same clothes he had worn when we left for Vegas almost a week earlier!

Grasshoppers

So... what made me consume two grasshoppers?

I am not talking about the kind that you might find in your backyard. I am talking about the cocktail named grasshopper. If you are not familiar with a grasshopper, that is understandable. The only two that I ever had were in 1968, and I have never known anyone to order one since then.

After I returned from my mission in Japan, I was dating a girl named Sandy. I should say I was trying to date a girl named Sandy because dating her was not going all that well. She was much more sophisticated than me, and she knew it. Sandy was a big fan of The Supremes. In the late '60s, Diana Ross and The Supremes were huge...as popular as The Beatles.

Sandy heard that The Supremes were going to be debuting their new song "Love Child" at the Coconut Grove, the very swanky nightclub at The Ambassador Hotel in Los Angeles. Demolished years ago, The Coconut Grove was the place to see and be seen. My boss, Bob, helped me get reservations for the late show one of the Fridays that The Supremes were performing. This date with Sandy was a significant investment in our relationship. If I remember correctly, the cover charge was $20 per person, not counting drinks or a tip. I figured the evening would set me back more than a week's pay.

The plan was for me to pick up Sandy and then for the two of us to have dinner in Hollywood. Because the show was so expensive, I figured we had to eat somewhere cheap. The problem was when I picked up Sandy, she was wearing her mother's costly, full-length mink coat. That coat was worth way more than the car I was driving. She was afraid to eat at any of the inexpensive places I suggested, worrying that someone might steal the mink.

So, we drove around Hollywood, killing time until it was time for the show at the Coconut Grove.

Now, getting back to the grasshopper....

I had never been to a nightclub, let alone a high-class place like The Coconut Grove. I wanted to make a good impression on Sandy and thought getting a good table would help. Checking in with the maître d', I knew I needed to tip, but I didn't know how to do that properly. I had a $5 bill in my hand, and I waved it around to make sure the maître d' saw it. He pointed to a spot on a large map, and one of his assistants took us to a cozy table for two right in the middle of the showroom. He politely accepted the $5 tip with a bow and a, "Thank you very much, sir."

Besides the cover charge, there was a two-drink minimum per person. Being a good Mormon at the time, I had no experience with cocktails. Sandy had more experience with drinks than me and said that I should order a grasshopper. An ounce of creme de menthe, creme de cacao, and cream make a grasshopper, a low alcohol content drink. The flavor was so intense that I could only sip my cocktail and didn't feel any effect from the booze.

Dianna Ross and The Supremes were great! The show was very high-energy and exciting and "Love Child" became a number-one hit. We had fun and enjoyed it, but I was honestly relieved to drop Sandy at home so that I would not have to worry about her mother's damn mink coat! I think that our big date was our last date! And, I have never had another grasshopper or dated anyone else who wore a mink coat!

NOIBN

Can you guess what NOIBN stands for?

N _____
O _____
I _____
B _____
N _____

It is not an abbreviation for the National Organization of Imbeciles, Buffleheads, and Nincompoops. And to answer the question you likely have on your mind; no, I am not a member. (I let my membership lapse several years ago.)

Returning from 2 ½ years in Japan, I attempted to resume my education. After meeting with a counselor at Long Beach City College, I learned that I only needed a couple of classes to complete my sophomore year. I also decided to change my major from Industrial Arts to Business. In order to get to work and open the camera store on time, I signed up for two early morning (7:00 a.m.) classes.

Having changed my major to business, you can probably understand my decision to take an accounting class. You may wonder, because I certainly do, why I took a National Motor Freight Classification class. It could have been that it was one of the few business classes at 7:00 a.m. that was still open.

The textbook for the National Motor Freight Classification class was the phone-book-like National Motor Freight Classification Guide. Today it costs $310, but if I remember correctly, it was $55 in 1970, about a week-and-a-half's pay.

The NMFC guide is used to determine the freight class for anything that might be shipped. Every commodity is listed, from avocados to zinc. There are 18 freight classes: 50 to 500. As an example, nuts, bolts, and steel rods are class 50 because they take up little space for how much they weigh, they are low value, and they are easy to ship. Ping pong balls, on the opposite end of the scale, are class 500 because they take up a lot of space for their weight and are easy to damage during shipping.

Once the freight class is known, the shipping cost can be quoted by a carrier or freight forwarder.

If a commodity is not listed in the guide, it can be classified as Not Otherwise Indexed by Name…NOIBN!

Honestly, I have never made use of what I learned in the class. The only benefit seems to be that I know what NOIBN stands for.

Oh, the course was pretty easy. I got an A which helped my grade point average.

Learning to Shoot Craps

Have you ever shot craps? Do you understand the rules and how to bet? I didn't until my future boss taught me!

Because my boss at Lakewood Camera liked to gamble, he seemed to wind up in Vegas frequently, with me tagging along.

On one of the many trips with Bob and his wife Joann, we met up with Bob's good friend and my future boss, Harry and his wife, Helen.

Bob, Joann, Harry, Helen, and I had seen Sinatra in the Copa Room at the Sands late Saturday night. (At least I am pretty sure it was Sinatra. The smoke was so thick in the showroom that I cannot be 100% sure! But it sounded like Sinatra!) After the show, Bob and Harry arranged for us to meet for breakfast Sunday morning before heading home.

We finished breakfast and still had a couple of hours to kill. Harry asked me if I knew how to play craps.

"No," I replied.

Harry then went on to explain in detail why craps was the only game in Vegas where the player had a reasonable chance to beat the house. "Let me show you how," he offered.

Not wanting to seem like a wimp, I said "Sure." But I worried that I only had about $12 in my pocket.

Even though it was Sunday morning, the casino was packed and very lively. Harry found a craps table with a lot of action. We elbowed in on one end, and he showed me how to place a bet on "The Line." Harry explained that if a seven or 11 were rolled, I would win my bet. A player at the opposite end of the table shook the dice, threw them down the table, and a four and three came up right in front of me. Wow, in seconds, my dollar had turned into two.

"Now if you want to improve your chance to win even more, you need to take the odds when a number is rolled," instructed Harry.

I left my two $1 chips on the Pass Line, and the player rolled the dice again. The number was not a seven or 11, so I didn't win. But it wasn't a two, three, or 12 either, so I didn't "crap out," or loose. I don't remember what the "point" was, but Harry told me to put $2 behind my $2 Pass Line bet to "take the odds." On the next play, the shooter rolled a seven, and the dealer took most of the money from the table, including my $4. I didn't like that! I was now out three bucks and down to nine.

Following Harry's lead, I put another $1 chip on the Pass Line and another $1 behind it to take the odds on whatever the point was. Harry then showed me how to win more money by making "place bets." I was worried about losing my $2, so I didn't follow Harry's lead this time and only played the Pass Line, taking the odds whenever I could.

My boss, mentor, and close friend Harry enjoyed craps!

We played for an hour or so, and at one point, I was up about $30, but that was before the table "went cold," and I lost it all! It was exciting to see Harry have small piles of chips spread all over the table. He seemed to be winning one of his bets every roll of the dice. He was always handing the dealer more chips to "buy" this or that bet, but to this day, I have no idea what that meant.

Bottom line...I learned to shoot craps. I lost $12, and I watched Harry lose more than $400.

I learned that craps is an easy game and can be a lot of fun. If a table is "hot" players will be crowded in close, enjoying free drinks, and many will be yelling and making a commotion. There are many ways to bet on a craps table, and that often intimidates the novice player. But craps is actually a simple game. You put your chips just about anywhere on the table, and after a while, the dealer will take them. When you run out of money, you're done!

Harry, my future boss and mentor, taught me how to shoot craps. Watching him lose $400, I learned an even more important lesson…even if you know how the game is played, you can lose your money!

New Year's Eve in Vegas

One way to get on the wrong side of your boss is to take his wife to Vegas for New Year's Eve.

You may remember that I worked for Lakewood Camera right out of high school. Two years after starting at the camera store, I went to Japan as a missionary, and 2 ½ years later I returned home. The day after getting home, I went back to work for Bob at Lakewood Camera.

Bob's wife Joann was beautiful. She had blond hair, blue eyes, and a great figure. Whenever Joann worked in the store, male customers hung around just to chat with her. She enjoyed the attention, and sales were better when she was there. She was good for business! Having two young children, Joann was not in the store often enough.

Besides a beautiful wife, Bob also had a girlfriend—referred to as Sam—on the side. One of my "jobs" was to fib to his wife when she called the store asking to talk to her husband when he was, in fact, out meeting his girlfriend.

Before Bob left for a rendezvous with Sam, he would instruct me to tell his wife he had to do this or that and would be back in an hour or two. It did not take long for me to realize that Joann knew that I was lying. She didn't seem to hold it against me, but it hurt me to lie to her, and I knew it hurt her to hear my lies. In spite of that, we became friends. We talked about the girls I was trying to date, and she always had a sympathetic ear and practical advice.

Bob was a big shot in the local Elks club, and the group was having a fancy New Year's Eve party. Bob came up with an excuse why he had to attend but could not take Joann. I knew what was going on, Joann knew what was going on, and Bob knew that both of us knew, but he didn't seem to care. He would be spending New Year's Eve partying with "Sam."

I was between girlfriends and Joann was faced with the prospect of spending New Year's Eve alone.

"What are you going to do?" she asked me about a week before New Year's Eve.

"I don't know," I replied. "You?"

"I just don't want to be sitting home while Bob is out partying with his girlfriend," said Joann.

I surprised myself when I asked, "Do you want to go to Vegas?"

"Sure, that would be fun," replied Joann.

The only rooms available on short notice for New Year's Eve were at Castaways, which was a small hotel and casino right across the street from The Sands. We drove up in Joann's station wagon, checked into the hotel, walked across the street to The Sands and hit the tables. We played blackjack at The Sands for a while but barely broke even. At the time, Circus Circus was one of the hot spots in Vegas, so we took a taxi to see if a change of venue would change our luck.

We found a blackjack table with three Japanese girls playing and decided to try our luck there. At the time my Japanese was still pretty good, having returned from Japan just a year earlier. As soon as we sat down, the three girls started talking about us in Japanese, assuming that we couldn't understand what they were saying.

From their conversation, they figured that Joann was older than me and wore a wedding ring while I did not. They thought that Joann might be having a fling with a younger man to spite her husband! One of the Japanese girls commented that Joann was so attractive that she could certainly do a lot better than me!

We played blackjack at the table with the Japanese girls for an hour or so before they ran out of chips and got up to leave.

Turning toward them, I commented, "*Anata no kai wa o kiite tanoshinde imasu. Gambate ne!*" (Translation: I enjoyed listening to your conversation. Good luck!).

Startled, each of the girls blushed, put their hands over their mouths, started giggling and hurried away from the table arm in arm.

Joann and I had fun New Year's Eve in Vegas. We gambled all night long and enjoyed lots of laughs. I think she may have forgotten about her husband partying with his girlfriend. We were both happy to be spending New Year's Eve with someone we liked rather than being alone at home.

After Joann and I went to Vegas, Bob and I never had quite the same relationship. I worked for him for about another year, but it was just not the same. I finally quit over a silly disagreement about where a trashcan should be kept (honest) and moved on.

I Do It Myself

Our oldest daughter, Aly, was (and is) headstrong. One of the things I remember her often saying when she was two or three was, "I do it myself."

Sometimes when we make such a statement, we wind up in situations that we would not have wound up in if we had been sensible and asked for help.

My best friend and roommate, George, had moved out of the apartment we shared on Cedar Avenue in Long Beach. I could not afford the place on my own and was going to move in with another friend. All the furniture in the small, second-story apartment was mine, so when George moved out, all he took were his clothes. That left me with everything else to move.

I am sure that if I had asked George or any of my other friends, they would have helped me move, but I didn't. Getting everything out of the apartment, down the stairs, and into the U-Haul truck was backbreaking work, but I did it. I did all of it, except for the very large and heavy refrigerator.

It was difficult, but with the refrigerator strapped securely to a furniture dolly, I made it out of the apartment and halfway down the stairs. Then I got stuck. Halfway down (or up), the stairway had a small landing before turning 180 degrees. With the refrigerator tipped back on the dolly wheels, there was not enough room to make the turn. I couldn't go down, and I could not go back up. I was stuck, blocking the stairway, and needed help.

Because we were moving out, I had turned off the phone service the day before. (This happened nearly 30 years before anyone had a cell phone.) I knocked on several of my neighbor's doors, and finally, one let me use their phone, but I couldn't reach any of my friends. In desperation, I called, my dad. He was home, and he came to help. The two of us were able to get the refrigerator turned so that it would go the rest of the way down the stairs and finally into the truck. The apartment that I was moving into had an elevator...phew.

Did I learn a lesson from this? Well, possibly not. My wife thinks that I don't ask for help often enough. I guess that I am still the kind of guy who thinks, "I do it myself!"

Working Late

I was not working late. The girl that I was trying to date, Cathy, seemed always to be working late.

As you recall, my boss, Bob, at Lakewood Camera had purchased Mercury Camera in Long Beach and promoted me to manager of his new store. Because business at Mercury was slow, I was often the only one working at the store, and I was happy to talk to anyone that came in.

Two customers that shopped at Mercury Camera were Cathy and Stacia, who lived nearby. They were both about my age, and I enjoyed it whenever they stopped in. They were both into photography, so we had a lot to talk about. I thought Cathy was pretty attractive, so I asked her out, and we started dating.

Going out on an actual date with Cathy involved a lot of patience on my part. She worked for her father doing bookkeeping at an auto upholstery shop in the Pico/Robertson area of Los Angeles. The shop closed at 5:00 p.m., which meant that she should have been back home in Long Beach by 6:30 or so. We would make a date for me to pick her up at her apartment, typically at 7:00 p.m. If she ever got home on time, which I can't remember ever happening.

While I waited for Cathy, I would pass the time hanging out with her roommate, Stacia. Usually, there would be a call from Cathy saying she would be very late... too late for us to go out.

With nothing better to do, Stacia and I would go to dinner. We often went to nearby Norm's coffee shop and almost always finished with a hot fudge cake for dessert. I wound up spending more time with Stacia than dating Cathy.

Over many months, Stacia and I became good friends. We did everything together and tried to include Cathy, but...Cathy always seemed to be working. Finally, Stacia and I admitted to each other that we had fallen in love, and we were married. Cathy was Stacia's Maid of Honor.

Stacia and I had two beautiful children, Chris and Aly. But, by the time Aly was about a year old, Stacia realized that she preferred someone of the same gender for her partner and we split up. We remain good friends, and she has always been a big part of our family.

Life drastically changes when you have a baby. A couple of years later, with a wife and two kids to support, it was now my turn to be the one working late!

Short Vegas Vacation

When I say short, I do not mean that we booked a week in Vegas and came home a day or two early. Our Vegas vacations were, in one word, short...hours not days.

I had quit working for Bob at Mercury Camera and took a job working for Bob's friends, Harry and Jerry, who owned Western Camera. I did not know it at the time, but I would work for Harry and Jerry for the next 27 years until they sold the business in 1977.

Western Camera was open six days a week. Monday through Thursday we were open from 9:00 a.m. until 6:00 p.m. Friday, we stayed open late...until 8:00 p.m. Saturday, we opened at 9:00 a.m. so we had 13 hours between closing Friday evening and opening Saturday morning. That was plenty of time to drive from Long Beach to Las Vegas, gamble for about four hours, drive back to Long Beach and open the store the next morning. Any time to sleep? NO!

Because I owned the best car, we generally took my 1970 yellow four-door Datsun 510. (Many may wonder what the heck a Datsun is. A few years after Nissan started selling vehicles in the U.S., they wanted a name that did not sound Japanese. So, a name that would be associated with all things American, Datsun, was chosen.)

To say my car was the "best" car should not cause you to believe that it was a particularly good car. It was in somewhat better running condition than the cars my friends owned. Typically, four or five of us made the trip. Our group included two or three of us who worked at the camera store and a couple of friends to fill up the car. And, with two in the front and three in the back, my little Datsun was packed and sat low on the springs.

As the clock ticked slowly toward 8:00 p.m., those of us working in the store did our clean-up early and had everything in order so that IF there were no customers, we could turn off the lights, lock up at precisely 8:00 p.m., and get on our way.

That never happened!

There was always one customer in the store that was either hanging around because they had nothing better to do on a Friday evening, or they wanted to make a major purchase, such as buying a roll of film and could not decide whether to buy a 24 or 36 exposure roll.

In those days, film was used to take photos. It came in two lengths, one to shoot 24 pictures and the other to shoot 36. When all the photos were shot, it was removed from the camera and taken to a camera store or drugstore to have the pictures developed and printed. You younger readers might think I am making this up, but I assure you that I am not! This was how photography was done in the early '70s. A few days later you went back to the store, picked up your prints, looked at them for a few minutes, then put them in a box, likely to never be seen again.

Often, the last customer of the day could not make up their mind, would keep us waiting 15 or 20 minutes, and wind up not buy anything. It was pretty damn frustrating.

After the lights were out, the security gate closed, the burglar alarm set, and the front door locked, we hit the road. We could typically make it to Vegas in about 4 ½ hours. This included a brief stop at Bun Boy in Baker California (Baker is home of the World's Tallest Thermometer...honest...Google it) for a bathroom break and to pick-up burgers for dinner as we continued toward Vegas.

On one of our trips, Stacia, the girl that would later become my first wife, was part of our little group. She was the roommate and best friend of a girl that I was trying to date, Cathy. I don't remember who else was on this trip, but we stopped at The

Tropicana about 1:00 a.m. to gamble because it was one of the first casinos you came to when heading north on The Strip. The casino was busy, full of energy, and we were all anxious to win some money.

One of the craps tables looked like fun with gamblers hooting and hollering, so we decided to give it a try. Stacia had never played craps and put a silver dollar (silver dollar coins were pretty common in Vegas at the time) on an area on the table called "the field." The shooter rolled a four, which meant that she won. The dealer picked up her silver dollar and replaced it with two $1 chips, but Stacia didn't realize that she had won her bet. Her dollar had become two dollars. Six rolls of the dice later the dealer leaned over toward her and said quietly, "Lady, you know that you have $128 sitting on the table?"

Surprised, Stacia quickly reached down and grabbed her pile of chips just before the shooter threw the dice and "sevened" out. What luck! Reading this now, you may think $128...no big deal. At that time, it was a huge deal. $128 was more than a week's pay for Stacia.

We had a great time that night, even though Stacia was the only big winner. And, if I remember correctly, she brought most of her winnings home.

We were still partying and having a blast about 4:30 a.m. when I started to gather our group to head back to Long Beach. I was driving, and was the only one awake, as the moon set in front of us and the sun rose behind heading down the interstate toward Baker. (Remember, this is the place with the World's Tallest Thermometer.) We opened the store just before 9:00 a.m. Not having had any sleep or time to shower and shave, I probably looked like hell. It was a very long day, but our short Vegas vacation had been worth it!

310 Termino

Mortgage lending regulations in the early '70s were much more lenient than they are today. You could likely not do now what we did then.

My wife was pregnant, and we felt that we needed more room than the very small house we were renting on Sixth Street in Long Beach. Stacia found a home that we both fell in love with, but we didn't have the money to buy it. By saying that we did not have the money, let me be clear:

1. We did not have a down payment
2. We did not have money for closing costs
3. We did not have enough income to qualify for the loan

These issues should have discouraged us, but they didn't.

310 Termino was a three-bedroom, two-bath, two-story home in Belmont Heights, a great residential area in Long Beach. It would be perfect for our growing family! A doctor was selling the home and asking $33,000. He had moved out, and the house had been vacant for a couple of months. It was within walking distance from my work, which was a huge advantage because we only had one car.

We wanted this house!

In the early '70s, there were no credit bureaus and no credit scores. To determine if you qualified for a loan, lenders called your employer and any credit references you had listed on your application. My wife and I knew that we were not earning enough to qualify for the loan we needed, so we fudged and listed both of our incomes as higher than they were. We felt confident that both of our employers would confirm the fictitious amounts if we asked them. Now we needed to find money for the down payment and closing costs.

The realtor told us that the doctor was very motivated to sell the home. I had the idea to offer the seller the full price he was asking, but with the provision that he would pay all our closing costs. We also asked for a black leather sofa that he had left in the living room. The realtor was surprised when the seller agreed. With a loan secured and the seller agreeing to pay all our closing costs, we needed to find the down payment.

Because we had lied about how much we earned and had a good credit report from my car loan, we were able to qualify for a 5 percent down payment. Great! Now we had to somehow come up with $1,650.

We would get back a $150 security deposit from the house that we were renting, and I had two weeks' vacation that I could cash out for $400. We would also have a month that we did not have to pay rent or a house payment which gave us another $150. My boss thought it was good that we were buying a home and agreed to advance me the $950.00 that we were short. I would have $50 withheld from my paycheck every other week until the personal loan was paid off.

We got the house!

We got the house, but we had no money! When I say that we had no money, we were truly house poor! We had a beautiful home in a great neighborhood but no money. My wife and I often had

Our former home today

to scrounge for change to buy diapers or put a few gallons of gas in our car. Thankfully, my mom and dad and our friends had us over for dinner often! It took about five months, but I got the $950 that we owed my boss paid off and that gave us some breathing room.

We loved our home on Termino, but the moving bug bit my wife. About two years later, we sold our house for $60,000 and the substantial profit we made allowed us to purchase an even nicer home in the very upscale Bixby Knolls area of Long Beach. But, not long after that, we split up.

In 2017, our old $33,000 house at 310 Termino in Long Beach sold for $875,000!

Christmas

What do you do when you don't have money to buy Christmas presents?

For my mother, now 91 years old, Christmas has always been her favorite time of the year. For years, she decorated every room in the house for the holidays, including the bathrooms. Her Christmas tree is always perfect.

Besides decorating, my mother also really enjoys the gift-giving. Christmas Eve, when the family gathered at her home, there were often as many as 10 presents for each person. Because there were so many gifts, each person's presents were wrapped in a different color or design gift wrap, and everyone had their own stack of presents.

My wife and I had just bought our first home, and we were broke. We were so short of money that we typically had to scrounge for change to put gas in our car. We had no money to buy presents, but we didn't want to show up on Christmas Eve empty-handed and disappoint my mom.

One evening, when we knew my parents were not going to be home, my wife and I went to their house and started looking through closets and drawers. We were searching for things that they might not miss and might not remember were theirs. An hour later, we had gathered eight to 10 items. We took our finds home and wrapped everything up as new presents for my mom and dad.

Christmas Eve, my wife and I were proud to walk into my folks' home each carrying a stack of beautifully wrapped gifts. As my mom opened her presents, she oohed and aahed about the great choices we made. One of her things that we wrapped was a sweater that we found deep in a dresser drawer, and we had never seen her wear. Opening the present, she exclaimed, "Oh, I love this sweater. I have one that is just like it, and it is one of my favorites."

Later that evening, my wife and I finally fessed-up to what we had done. Because of the excitement and overall mayhem, neither my mom nor dad understood what had just happened. It wasn't until a few days later that my mother finally realized that all her gifts from us that year were her own things.

Dr. Z

James Bond movies were wildly popular in the late '60s and early '70s. Several films featured deranged villains with the title of doctor. The Dr. Z that I am writing about was not a character in a James Bond story.

What do you do when you don't have medical insurance or any savings, and a baby is due?

Having purchased a house that we could not afford, my wife and I barely had enough money for our day-to-day expenses. Our financial situation would only get worse when my wife stopped working because our first child, Chris, was born.

My boss's son, Jerry, was only a couple years older than I was, and we worked together in the camera store every day. When there were no customers, we often talked. I didn't ask Jerry for help, but he knew we were overextended with our house and figured that I needed help because my wife was growing more pregnant every day.

One of Jerry's great traits is that he is genuinely interested in other people. Because of that, he has always had a lot of friends. One of his friends in the early '70s was Dr. Z, an Ob/Gyn practicing in Orange County. Dr. Z was also a customer, so I knew him, and often helped him when he came into the store.

I remember the day when Dr. Z was in the camera store talking to Jerry. Motioning me over, Jerry said that Dr. Z was willing to help by caring for my wife and delivering our baby.

I did not know exactly what this meant, but Dr. Z said, "Don't worry about any charges for my services. I am happy to help you and your wife out." Handing me his card he said, "Have your wife call my office and set-up an appointment."

During one of the appointments, Dr. Z had an x-ray taken of my wife and our baby. The quality of the X-ray images was not very good (this was years before ultrasound was available for fetal imaging) and seemed to show that our baby had an enlarged head. A few days later, Dr. Z brought the x-ray into Western Camera to show it to me and cautioned that our baby might have Downs Syndrome.

My wife and I were devastated. We didn't know what to do but accept the fact that the baby we had been looking forward to might require a lot of extra care. We both had no thoughts other than we would love and care for our baby no matter his condition.

A couple of months later, and after more than 24 hours of labor, Dr. Z delivered our baby by Cesarean Section. He was perfect in every way. The umbilical cord was in such a position as it made our son's head look much larger than what was normal in the x-ray image. It was also the reason for the long labor and C-section birth. Chris was jaundiced, so he had to stay in the hospital for several days, but otherwise he was a perfect baby boy! My wife and I were overjoyed!

While everything with our baby turned out perfectly, we were still anxious about medical bills. Because Chris was born by C-section, an anesthesiologist and second surgeon assisted Dr. Z. and, my wife was in the hospital longer because of the surgery. We were worried that large medical bills we couldn't afford to pay would be coming.

We never received a bill from the hospital or any of the other doctors.

I am not sure how Dr. Z pulled this off, but our out-of-pocket costs for our baby were zero! We had to do something for Dr. Z to show our appreciation.

I asked Jerry for ideas, and he asked, "Have you ever seen Dr. Z's car?"

For a well-known physician, Dr. Z drove what many would consider a "junker!" The paint was so severely oxidized that you couldn't tell what the original color was. Two hubcaps were missing, the antenna was broken in half, and the landau top was in shreds! (A landau top was a fixed roof, covered with cloth or simulated leather to make the car look like a convertible…weird!) His car looked like crap.

From an earlier chapter, you may remember Cathy, who I was trying to date before I married Stacia. Cathy's father owned an auto upholstery shop and my wife worked there part time. Besides upholstery work, the shop also repaired landau tops. We asked Dr. Z if we could take his car for a few days to have the top repaired. He seemed thrilled that we would do this for him.

About a week later we brought Dr. Z's car back to him. It looked like a different car. The shop had replaced the torn landau top, installed a new antenna, replaced the missing hubcaps, buffed out the oxidized paint and completely detailed the interior and exterior of the car. It looked brand new!

Dr. Z was surprised and seemed amazed at the transformation. He had a big smile on his face as he walked around the car examining it carefully.

"How much do I owe you?" he asked. That was the kind of guy he was.

"It was our pleasure and the least that we could do," my wife and I replied in unison.

Two years later, Dr. Z delivered our daughter Alyxandria. Once again, there was no bill for either his services or the hospital. Jerry suggested that we buy Dr. Z a new stereo as a thank you, which we did.

Dr. Z passed away in Naples, Florida, in 2015, after having delivered over 5,000 babies, including two of ours! Thank you again, Dr. Z.

Dirty Pictures

In the '70s, photos were shot on film, and the film was then taken somewhere (typically a camera store or drugstore) to be developed. The store sent the film out to a photo lab who did the actual work. Depending on the type of film, you either got back prints or slides.

At Western Camera, we primarily sent film to Kodak for processing. When a Kodak lab developed slide film (Kodachrome—as Paul Simon so famously sang about—or Ektachrome—I don't think anyone ever sang about Ektachrome!), the finished slides (either 24 or 36 per roll) were delivered in small yellow boxes. I still have many of these little yellow boxes filled with memories from the past.

To offer something different than other stores, Western Camera also offered the service of a local photo lab. They did excellent work, comparable to Kodak, but differentiated their service by delivering the finished slides in PVC sheets that were about the size of notebook paper. Twenty slides fit on each page, and unlike boxed slides, it was easy to hold up a sheet of slides and see all the images.

One of our employees, Tim, was offering a customer the option of this service and to show the advantage, he pulled a random sheet of slides from those waiting to be picked up. Tim laid the sheet of slides on a lightbox so that the customer could see the advantage. I was only a few feet away and noticed the customer bent over to get a closer look. As he stared at the sheet of slides, he looked surprised, then shocked. Tim realized that the photos he pulled out as an example were of a naked couple engaging in sex. Embarrassed, he grabbed the sheet of slides, put them back into the envelope and suggested that Kodak processing might be the better choice.

The Building is Tilting!

California is known for earthquakes. During the 1994 devastating 6.7 magnitude Northridge earthquake, thousands of buildings were damaged and left tilting on their foundations.

When I went to work for Western Camera and Hi-Fi in 1970, it was a small retail store on Anaheim Street in Long Beach, California, that sold cameras and hi-fi systems. Hi-fi was an acronym for high fidelity, which is the type of sound you wanted if you were into music in the early '70s.

The store owners, Harry and Jerry, had built Western Camera into the leading camera store in the area. We sold all the best brands. If you were into photography and lived in the greater Long Beach area, you shopped at Western Camera.

A few years after I went to work at Western Camera, Jerry wanted to expand our business by selling film and photo supplies to local hospitals. Rather than wait for them to need something and come into our store (it would be another 40 years before you could buy online from Amazon.com), he pushed me to go out and sell to local hospitals. He had to push me because:

1. I had never done this before
2. I had no idea what I was supposed to do
3. Making sales calls to hospitals frightened me

Our sales to hospitals started slow, and for the first year, we were able to keep the stuff we sold (primarily Kodak and Polaroid film) in a small storeroom in the back of the camera store. As our sales grew, and they grew very rapidly, so did the need for storage space. We had floor-to-ceiling shelves built in the storeroom, but this only helped the situation for about six months.

Realizing that we need a lot more space, Harry and Jerry, decided to dig up the parking lot and put in a basement warehouse that would be as large as the entire store. The one dissenting vote to this plan was Harry's wife, Helen. She worried that digging a huge hole in the parking lot right next to the building would cause damage to the store might cause the whole building to fall into the

Excavation of Western Camera parking lot to build basement warehouse
hole.

One of the guys that I worked with was Scott. Like me, he enjoyed pulling pranks on others. Helen had a desk in our small office, and Scott and I decided to tilt her desk toward the excavation a little at a time. To do this, we put a single penny under each of the back legs of her desk each day before she arrived.

Pennies are not very thick, so the tilting of her desk was very gradual. Day by day, Helen's desk tilted a little more until finally, Helen laid a pencil on her desk and it quickly rolled off and onto the floor. Her fear of the building tilting and falling into the excavation was confirmed!

In a panic, she screamed at the top of her voice, "Dear (meaning her husband and our boss Harry) THE BUILDING IS TILTING!"

Scott and I were laughing so hard that neither of us heard how Harry replied. Seeing us bent over laughing, Helen figured out Scott and I were behind this. She gave us the stink-eye and the cold-shoulder for the next week or so, but that was the extent of our punishment.

When the excavation was finished, we had a large basement warehouse and a new parking lot on top of it. There was no damage to our building either from the construction or from a small earthquake that we had during construction.

Picking Up Girls

Well, this is actually about picking up one specific girl.

My first wife and I had separated, and it was one of my nights to have the kids. I wanted to see the new Peter Sellers movie, "The Pink Panther," so I got the diaper bag ready, a bottle for my one-year-old daughter Aly, some stuffed animals, baby blankets and loaded everything into the car. We got to the drive-in theater while it was still light so my three-year-old son, Chris, could play on the swings and rides in the kids' area right next to the refreshment stand.

Many who read this will have no idea what I am talking about. When I was a kid, people with kids who wanted to see a movie went to a drive-in theater. Very seldom were young kids taken to regular indoor theaters where they might fuss and make some unwelcome noise. Families with kids went to a drive-in theater, that's just what you did.

Drive-in theaters were outside and had a huge screen and rows of parking spaces slightly angled so the parked cars could see the big screen. Between each car was a pole that had a speaker attached to it with a long cord. You could unhook the speaker from its pole and bring it into your vehicle so you could hear the movie. The sound quality was not very good, and the movie picture quality was not very good, but these were the days when color television was still a new technology, and tablets and smartphones were decades in the future.

Drive-in theaters had play areas to attract families with young children. Some would even have pony rides. I think the idea was to sell more tickets by getting kids to beg their parents to go to the drive-in theater.

"The Pink Panther" was playing at the Circle Drive-In theater in Long Beach. (The drive-in is long gone, having been demolished in 1985.) After finding a spot to park my gold Ford Fairlane (Yes, my car was a gold Ford Fairlane, but that's another story), I took my kids to the play area. I was holding my one-year-old daughter on my lap as my three-year-old son played on one of those contraptions that spin around as fast as someone will push it.

Not 10 feet from me, I noticed a very attractive woman sitting on one of the benches eating Animal Crackers. She had a small dog on a leash and looked like a young mother. She was not wearing a wedding ring, so I thought she might be single, like me. I was certainly interested in her, and I tried to see which child or children were hers.

"Which one is yours?" I asked.

She looked at me, smiled, and said she didn't have any children. "I just wanted to see 'The Pink Panther.'"

Her reply caught me off guard, and I did not know what to say. Just then, my son fell off the contraption he was playing on, and I had to go and take care of him. He wasn't hurt but did cry for a few minutes as a three-year-old is supposed to do.

By the time I was able to refocus my attention on "The Girl That Ate Animal Crackers and Didn't Have Kids," she was gone!

The movie—actually, the cartoons (one or more cartoons were shown before movies at drive-in theaters) were starting so I gathered my two kids and headed back to our car. Walking back, I noticed the girl sitting alone in a green Datsun only a few cars away from ours. I put my kids in the back seat of the car, made sure they would be OK for a minute or two and struck-out to talk to the girl, hoping I would not strike out.

It was a warm evening, and her car window was down.

"Hi, again," I said.

"Hi, again," was her reply. She was smiling, so I decided to press on.

"Would you like to see the movie with my kids and me?" I asked.

"Can I bring my dog?" she asked in reply.

It wasn't until we got back to my car that I introduced myself to Sharon. During the "Previews of Coming Attractions" we chatted, and I learned that she was a respiratory technologist at Memorial Hospital in Long Beach. Having worked there a few years earlier, we knew some of the same people, so we connected quickly. We both enjoyed the movie, and the car was filled with our laughter as my kids and Sharon's dog slept in the back seat.

I was successful in picking-up Sharon, but that was the only time I picked up a girl at a drive-in movie theater. Sharon and I dated for about six months but longer-term our relationship didn't work out.

I wonder if I was the only guy to pick her up at a drive-in movie theater.

Picking Up Girls – Part 2

Being divorced and single in my mid-20s, of course I wanted to meet girls. And I thought, taking co-ed tennis lessons might be a way to do that.

I signed up for a beginner's tennis class at El Dorado Park through the Long Beach Recreation Department.

To get ready for the class, and my new lifestyle as a tennis player, I purchased a Jimmy Connors tennis racquet, new white tennis shoes, and a bright red warm-up suit. I showed up for the first class, and there must have been about 15 of us. The instructor was a guy named Jim. I stood out in my brand-new red outfit, which I regretted.

At the first class there appeared to be quite a few single ladies. I eagerly went to class the next week and scoped out those that I found attractive. Jim matched us up with different partners several times during each lesson. When I was paired up with a girl that I thought was attractive, I would start up a conversation and at some point, ask them out. Without exception, each made some comment about being busy and needing to check their schedule.

"I'll let you know next week at class," was their polite, convenient and evasive reply.

So, what happened? I never got a direct answer, but each girl that I asked out answered me by not coming back to class! This was not all bad because as one girl then another stopped coming to class, those of us left had more individualized instruction from the teacher.

I showed up for what I remember as the eighth or ninth class, and it was only the instructor and me. As the ladies stopped coming to class, so did some of the other guys. I wondered if the reason the other guys were there was to meet girls too? Fewer girls seemed to equal fewer guys.

Jim and I were doing some volley drills, and he lamented that classes always thinned out, but this was his first class ever, where so many had stopped coming. He asked me what I thought he was doing wrong!

After hitting the ball back and forth in silence for a few minutes, my guilty conscience got the best of me.

"It's my fault," I blurted.

Startled, Jim grabbed the ball that I had returned and asked, "What do you mean?"

I confessed what I had done—asking girl after girl out, causing his class to shrink to one! Expecting Jim to at least say that was not appropriate, I was surprised when he said, "I've got an idea."

He asked me to join the intermediate tennis class the next week.

I showed up the next week, and Jim introduced me as a student from his beginners' class that belonged with the intermediate group. During class, he called a beautiful blond over and introduced me to my next wife.

Clean Toilets

When I started working at Western Camera in 1970, there were two tiny bathrooms. Each had a toilet and small sink. We had a cleaning service come once a week, but the bathrooms got pretty disgusting between those cleaning visits. Because I like a clean restroom, I started cleaning both bathrooms each morning. I don't think it took me more than 15 minutes, and for at least a few hours, we had clean restrooms.

Harry, the owner of Western Camera, and my boss, often saw me cleaning the bathrooms and called me into his office one day. "I didn't hire you to clean toilets," Harry said. "But, it shows me that you care about the company."

Four years later, after Western Camera had grown from about 15 to about 60 employees, Harry promoted me to General Manager. I have often thought that cleaning those bathrooms wound up helping my career significantly.

In 1983, we expanded our business by opening a distribution center in Houston, Texas. On one of my early visits to check on things, my flight was more than an hour late. I landed in Houston and didn't take the time to use the restroom at the airport before getting on the shuttle to pick up a rental car. Because I was in a hurry, I also skipped using the bathroom at Hertz, and got on the road right away. Having to pee very badly, I squirmed in my seat for the hour it took to drive to our warehouse. By the time I got there, it felt like my bladder was ready to burst.

The warehouse bathroom was filthy!

After I relieved myself, I rummaged around, found some cleaning supplies, and about a half hour later I had the restroom spotless. The warehouse manager made some excuses for why the bathroom had not been clean. My reply was, "Don't worry about it."

Because of some other issues, I fired the warehouse manager about a month later.

Over the next few years, we opened warehouses in Chicago, Philadelphia, and Orlando. Somehow, word spread to the warehouse managers that the GM (me) expected bathrooms to be kept clean. I was never disappointed in that regard again.

Holiday Inn

This story is not about an intentional prank, rather a series of events that may have seemed like a prank played on an unsuspecting engineer visiting from Germany.

To set-the-stage for this story, I need to explain a little about what had happened to Western Camera's business as medical sales exploded. To grow our business, I was making sales calls to hospitals almost daily. When I handed my Western Camera and Hi-Fi business card to a customer, the response was often, "We don't need any cameras or hi-fi equipment."

It quickly became apparent that we needed a new name for our medical supply business.

We came up with a long list of possible names, but each was rejected as either being inappropriate or already in use. Finally, we chose the name of Harry's first grandson, and Jason Marketing became our new name. (The grandson's name was Jason, not marketing!)

In the early '70s, heart catheterization was a relatively new tool used to diagnose heart disease. During the procedure, a catheter is inserted into the femoral artery and guided into the heart. Once the catheter is in the heart, radio-opaque dye (a dye that shows up as black on an x-ray) is injected through the catheter. Later, a cardiologist reviews the film and can see arteries where blood flow was reduced or even blocked.

Cardiologists often complained that the quality of the film was so poor that they could not see how severe a blockage was. The Kodak motion picture film used to record the procedure was often blamed for the poor quality.

Having a background in photography, we understood that the poor image quality, often described as graininess, was not caused by the film, but rather by the part of the x-ray system called the image intensifier. Technically this was known as quantum-mottle. We also understood that changes to exposure and how the film was processed (developed) could improve the image quality by reducing the apparent graininess.

To promote our business and help hospitals improve the diagnostic quality of their Cath-lab films, we held the first Cardiovascular Cine Roentgenography Symposium (quite a mouthful!) at Long Beach Memorial Hospital.

There was a great deal of interest in improving the quality of cath lab imaging, and we were able to enlist prominent physicians and suppliers to present lectures and demonstrations at our meeting. One of our suppliers sent an engineer from Germany, and he gave a very informative presentation.

The evening after the symposium, the company hosted a dinner at the Holiday Inn. There were about 25 guests at the diner with half being from the company and the other half being those who had made presentations, including the German engineer.

Just before 10:00 p.m., our waitress told us that the restaurant was closing, and we had to move to the bar if we were going to continue our affair. The German engineer thanked us for the dinner and drinks. He said that he had to go to bed because he would be leaving the hotel at 5:00 a.m. for an early flight from Los Angeles.

It was nearly 2:00 a.m. when our server told us that the bar was closing and if we wanted anything else, this would be the last call. One of the guys, Mitch, had gone down to his room and another one of the guys, Lee, figured that Mitch would want another drink.

"I'm going to call Mitch. Does anyone know his room number?" Lee asked. The best anyone could come up with was that his room was on the 9th floor. Lee found a house phone and started dialing rooms on the 9th floor beginning with room 901.

I settled our bill and was leaving to go home. Getting off the elevator on the ground floor, I was very surprised to see the German engineer sitting in the lobby dressed for the day with his large suitcase in front of him.

I asked, "What are you doing here?"

"My wake-up call came, and therefore my ride to the airport will be here shortly."

"What was your room number?" I asked.

"904. Why?" he asked.

I did not have the heart to tell him that it was only 2:30 in the morning!

Mitch's room was on the 8th floor.

Brand Loyalty

What makes you loyal to a particular brand?

My second wife, Phyllis, was a travel agent when Marriott opened their 100th hotel, a gorgeous beachfront property on Maui in 1983. The hotel (now called Marriott's Maui Ocean Club) had a promotion for travel professionals. Phyllis was able to book a complimentary room for the two of us and our one-year-old son, Andrew.

We had a beautiful ocean-front room with a large lanai overlooking the beach. It was perfect! It was the first time I had stayed in a Marriott hotel, and I was impressed with both the property and the excellent service.

I forgot to bring a book from home and found myself with nothing to read. I was going to see if they had any books in the gift shop, but before I did that, I found a book in the nightstand. It was "Marriott: The J. Willard Marriott story," a book about the company's founder and the history of Marriott. I read a few pages and figured that it would do. As I read while we relaxed on the beach, I remember being fascinated and impressed by Marriott's history. Strange as it may seem, I said to myself, "I am going to stay at 100 Marriott hotels."

That quirky statement led me on a very enjoyable 18-year journey. I finally reached my goal of staying at 100 different Marriott full-service hotels in February 2001.

They say old habits die hard, and that must be especially true for me. After I reached my goal of staying at 100 different Marriott hotels, I couldn't stop! I continued to find new hotels to add to my list. My last new Marriott was Palm Beach Gardens in Florida in June 2015. It was number 161.

My wife, Teresa, and I were married at the Costa Mesa Marriott, and I was staying at the Springfield Marriott on 9/11. Our granddaughter, Layne, has already shown her hotel preference!

Two of my most memorable Marriott experiences both happened at the Marriott Marquis San Diego Marina hotel. My second wife, Phyllis, and I were having dinner  in the hotel with our two children. Drew and Kelly were seven and five. After we finished dinner, our waiter asked if he could "borrow" our kids to give my wife and I a little time alone. He took them across the restaurant to a soft serve ice cream machine and helped them make sundaes. Instead of bringing them right back, they got to sit at their own table and enjoy their desserts. They loved it. My wife and I loved it.

Years later my wife, Teresa, and I were checking to the same hotel. As the front desk associate was handing us our room keys, he asked, "Is there anything else I can do for you?"

Joking, I said, "A bottle of champagne would be nice."

About fifteen minutes after settling into our room, there was a knock at the door. A room service waiter rolled a table with an ice bucket and a half-bottle of champagne into the room. Along with the champagne was a note from the front desk associate thanking us for choosing Marriott. Outstanding!

What started as a seemingly frivolous goal wound up giving me and our family many great memories and has made me a huge fan of the Marriott brand.

The Art of Negotiation

Donald Trump already used the phrase, "The Art of the Deal" in his 1987 book, so this chapter describing how to get the best deal when buying a car is called "The Art of Negotiation."

To get the lowest price when purchasing a new car, it is essential to show the salesperson that you don't care if you leave without making a deal. Showing any amount of enthusiasm will definitely hurt your chance of getting a good price.

My wife and I - the one I met at tennis lessons - had two children and we were shopping for a minivan to hold our family of four plus the dog. The idea of a minivan was brand new. I think the '84 Plymouth Voyager was the first mini-van and we thought this would be the perfect vehicle for our little family. We left the kids with my wife's parents and headed out to shop for one.

When we arrived at the car lot, there were at least a half-dozen salesmen—all men—lined up and ready to sell us a new car. We asked to see Voyagers and were immediately discouraged with a dialog like "They are really in high demand and hard to come by. There is a waiting list, and they are going for about a grand more than the sticker price."

This statement seemed very odd to me because I could see more than a dozen brand new Voyagers lined up facing the street. The salesman finally relented, and after both my wife and I test drove the car, we pretty much decided that we were going to buy one on the spot. Now it was my job to negotiate the price.

It was a hot day, and I figure that it would be better for me to negotiate standing outside in the blazing Southern California sun, rather than in the salesman's air-conditioned cubicle. I didn't need the extended warranty, the dealer's special protective finish, the door guards, or to spend the extra $1,000 because "there is more demand for these cars than the factory can fill."

Using Trump-like negotiating skills, I had gotten down to the sticker price! Now, my job was to try to shave at least a few hundred dollars off that.

My wife had been wandering around, looking at all the Voyagers on the lot. She came over and said that she knew which one she wanted.

I think that I said something like, "Honey, I'm not sure we can afford what they are asking."

Pointing to a light-blue one she said, "I don't care what the price is. I want that one."

Her comment and the salesman's knowing grin ended any further negotiations. We drove off in the powder blue Voyager, and it served our family well for years.

When negotiating a purchase, it is highly recommended not to allow the salesperson to hear, "I don't care what the price is!"

Christmas II

As I said in a previous chapter, Christmas is my mother's favorite time of year. Christmas Eve the whole family gathered at her house to exchange presents, have a wonderful Italian dinner, and have dozens of photos taken.

One year, the day after Christmas, my mom realized she had misplaced the two rolls of film shot the night before. She was frantic, so I went over to help her look for the film. We searched through the house and several large bags of trash but didn't find the missing film. Losing her Christmas photos upset my mom so much that she was crying. I think that I said something like, "Mom, the film didn't disappear. It will turn up."

A day or two later, the film had still not turned up. Christmas photos were so important to my mom that she called everyone (this was years before email, text messaging, or Facebook) and said that we were going to redo Christmas Eve. She set a date for the middle of January and told everyone they were expected to be there dressed as they had been for Christmas Eve.

I remember being asked at work what I had planned for the upcoming weekend. "We're going to Christmas Eve dinner at my mom's house," I said.

"Wasn't that a few weeks ago," was the next question.

Our second Christmas Eve was a success. Presents had been rewrapped, my mom made another family dinner, dozens of photos were taken, and we all had a great time.

A day or two later when my mom was going to take the pictures in for developing, she somehow wound up with a couple of extra rolls of film. Picking up the prints a few days later, she realized that she had both the original Christmas Eve photos and those from the do-over evening.

Every year after, until my mom got her first digital camera, we took extra care to make sure used rolls of film were not lost!

A Bag of Cash

Before I can explain why I sat at my desk guarding a brown paper bag with $40,000 in cash in it, I need to describe what the "Grey Market" in the '70s was.

Dealing in the Grey Market was not illegal, as compared to trading in the Black Market, but it was at least suspicious and very risky.

Grey Market refers to goods which are sold outside of the manufacturers authorized sales channel. Dealing in the Grey Market was risky because profit margins were very small. Any mistake would likely wipe out what little profit there might have been.

Dr. Mark XXXX was a Canadian dentist (HONEST!) who somehow got involved in purchasing Grey Market goods in the U.S. and importing them into Canada. One of the products he handled was photographic film. I am not sure how he got hooked up with Jason Marketing, but after some negotiations, we began selling him huge quantities of Polaroid film. When I say huge quantities, I am talking truckloads!

Besides Polaroid film, hospitals were purchasing large quantities of videotape, which was used to record ultrasound studies. A typical dealer might order a half dozen cases of videotape from the manufacturer, but we were ordering hundreds of cases at a time. Purchasing in such large quantities gave us a small price advantage.

Somehow, we got hooked up with a guy who owned a bunch of video stores in Southern California. (In their heyday, there used to be more video stores than McDonald's restaurants.) Harry or Jerry struck a deal to sell him videotape for less than he could purchase it from the manufacturer. I think we were going to make a dime a tape. The deal was for 1,000 cases of tape, and the price he agreed to required him to pick up the tape from us and pay in cash.

On the day of the deal, we had the cases of tape stacked on pallets in the warehouse. The customer was supposed to arrive at 11:00 a.m. but called to say he was running late. Usually, Harry or Jerry would handle the finances of these Grey Market transactions, but they had to be somewhere else that afternoon. The customer finally showed up and we completed the deal in my office.

My role consisted of carefully counting the cash he had brought...2,000 $20 bills and giving the warehouse the OK to load the pallets of VHS tape into his waiting bobtail truck, which should have been easy.

It was then that my dilemma began. What was I going to do with the $40,000 in cash until my bosses returned? The money was bulky and was way too much to stuff in my pockets.

I couldn't go to lunch carrying a bag of cash, and I was starving. I couldn't entrust the money to anyone else either. When I had to pee, I had to take the money with me into the men's room. Except for the one bathroom break I sat in my office most of the afternoon guarding the bag of $20s until Harry and Jerry got back and I handed it off to them. Phew!

I think this was one of our last Grey Market deals, which was fine with me. I had no desire to be responsible for stacks of $20 bills again.

Girl Scout Days

Yes, I was a Girl Scout!

Our youngest daughter, Kelly, was a Girl Scout and her mom, my second wife Phyllis, was the troop leader. My wife recommended that I become an official Girl Scout so that the organization's insurance would cover us if I was driving girls to a scouting event, so I joined.

A few weeks after becoming a Girl Scout, I received my official "Certificate of Membership," which I carried proudly in my wallet.

At the time that Kelly was a Girl Scout, there were no ATMs or debit cards. Credit cards weren't commonly used for day-to-day expenses. When you bought something, you either paid cash or wrote a check. When you wrote a check, most stores asked for two forms of identification. It was fun for me to hand the checker my driver's license and my Girl Scout membership card. Without fail, they would look at the card, look at me, then question how I could be a Girl Scout and not be a girl.

It was always good for a laugh!

My Valet

I woke up on the morning of my 40th birthday to a very tall man standing next to our bed, holding my underwear for me. To say that I was startled was an understatement!

"Are these the underwear you prefer this morning, Sir?" asked the gentleman with a strong British accent.

Not fully awake, I demanded, "Who the hell are you?"

"First, let me wish you a very happy birthday, Sir. I am Giles, your valet, of course."

This story really starts in 1981, when I saw the movie "Arthur" starring Sir Dudley Moore and Sir John Gielgud as his butler. Moore plays a wealthy alcoholic playboy who couldn't get through a day without the assistance of his loyal butler, Hobson. Whenever I was having grooming issues or trying to figure out what to wear, I would jokingly tell my wife that my life would certainly be easier if I had a butler or valet. Now, back to the morning of October 12, 1985.

After helping me get dressed (which was itself a unique experience), Giles inquired if I was ready for breakfast. I remember coffee, orange juice, and a very large blueberry muffin. The kitchen table had been properly set, of course.

"Would you like your muffin cut in the English or American manner," Giles inquired. Not knowing the difference, I chose English, which turned out to be cut from the top down.

Giles warmed and then expertly cut and buttered the muffin and presented it to me on a plate.

After breakfast, Giles cleaned up the kitchen then bid my wife and I farewell, saying, "It has been my pleasure serving you this morning."

After Giles left, my wife told me of her call to the agency. She was told that wives typically request strippers or French maids for similar occasions. The company called back to confirm that she really wanted a male actor to play a valet instead of a scantily dressed French maid.

Come to think of it; I might have enjoyed my birthday morning even more if my wife had requested one of those scantily clad French maids!

The Big Fight

No, this story is not about the 1991, "Battle of the Ages," the WBC, WBA, and IBC championship fight between Evander Holyfield and George Foreman held in Atlantic City. (Holyfield won by a unanimous decision of the judges.)

This story is about an argument between me and my wife. It should not have been a fight at all, and I will take full responsibility for escalating it from a simple disagreement to bad feelings that lasted all day. If you are reading this Phyllis, I am sorry.

Phyllis, Andrew (now referred to as Drew), Kelly, and I were driving somewhere. Seemingly, out of the blue, my wife asked our kids, "What's the difference between an airplane and a helicopter?"

"A helicopter has wings that go around and around," responded 8-year old Kelly.

"No, a helicopter doesn't have wings," corrected my wife. That's when I felt I had no choice but to speak up.

"Kelly is right. The proper name for a helicopter is rotary wing aircraft," I said firmly.

The subsequent argument between my wife and I escalated and pretty much put a damper on whatever we were doing the rest of the day.

But Kelly was right.

BF II

Or Big Fight #2. I write about this because in hindsight I think it is pretty funny, but neither my wife nor I thought it funny at the time. I will take full responsibility for escalating a minor disagreement into a full-blown argument that ruined another day.

Leaving our home in Fountain Valley, we were heading "down" the 405 Freeway toward San Diego. We had just gotten on the freeway at Magnolia and had only driven a few miles when my wife asked the kids which way we were going.

"East," replied Kelly.

"No, we are going South," corrected my wife.

We had just passed Harbor Boulevard, and I corrected my wife saying "No, Kelly is right. We're going East."

While the 405 Freeway (aka the San Diego Freeway) heads in generally a southeast direction, the section that we were on heads almost directly East.

My wife offered an argument or two supporting the fact that in general, we were heading South. I should have dropped it, but I did not. Once again, as in the chapter "The Big Fight," I now apologize.

But Kelly was right, again!

That was, I think, my first indication that Kelly has an extraordinarily good sense of direction...like her older sister Aly...and like me.

But, was it worth it for me to ruin the day with another big fight over something so trivial? Not really!

Cold Turkey

My second wife and I had separated about six months earlier, and I was living in the Harbor Lights apartment complex not far from work. I had not taken much from our Irvine home except for my clothes.

My apartment was sparingly furnished, and I had a little refrigerator, often referred to as a "dorm fridge." Besides not having a freezer, it didn't have room for even the smallest turkey.

My oldest daughter, Aly, learned that I was going to be alone on Thanksgiving and said that she didn't have plans and would have dinner with me. With neither of us in the mood to cook, we went out for Thanksgiving dinner.

Parking for Harbor Lights residents was in the basement, which is also where the trash dumpsters were located. When a resident wanted to discard a large object, they would haul it down to the basement and put it next to one of the dumpsters.

Coming back from dinner, Aly noticed a refrigerator next to one of the trash bins. "Dad, look at that. Let's check it out."

Needing a full-size refrigerator, but not wanting to haul one up three stories only to discover that it did not work, I got an extension cord and plugged it in. We came back about a half-hour later, and it seemed to be working because the freezer was cold. But the refrigerator was filthy.

By filthy, I mean that it was dirty inside and out. There was mold growing in the corners and on the rubber door seals. Stuff had spilled inside, and it had grown into something disgusting. And, it smelled awful.

"Dad, we can clean this up. Let's get it up to your apartment," my daughter said. Getting it up to my apartment was not an easy task.

We didn't have a furniture dolly or any other apparatus to help us. The refrigerator was way too heavy for us to carry it, so we scooted it. We scooted it into the elevator, which was not too difficult because the floor was concrete, and we rode up to the third floor.

The hallway and my apartment were carpeted, so scooting would not work. By tipping the refrigerator up on one corner at a time, we "walked" it to my front door. This took us quite a while because we had to stop to catch our breath. Finally, we got it through the front door and into my small kitchen. Phew!

We spent the next couple of hours cleaning the fridge. When we finished, it was spotless and looked like new. We plugged it in while we were cleaning, so it had gotten cold. We transferred the few things from my mini fridge to my new full-size one. If I would have had this fridge a few days earlier, I might have cooked a turkey instead of going out and would have been able to keep the leftovers.

The rescued fridge worked perfectly for the 4 ½ years I lived there. When I moved out, I left it in the apartment and left it spotless.

I wonder if the people that cleaned the units between tenants hauled it back down to the trash area.

Crumb Cake Marinara

A delicious twist on a classic. The addition of Marinara sauce gives this version a unique Italian flavor and festive look.

Cake Ingredients
1/2 cup butter, room temp
1 cup granulated sugar
3/4 tsp table salt
2 tsp vanilla extract
3 large eggs
1 cup Marinara sauce
1 1/2 cups flour
1/8 tsp baking soda

Topping Ingredients
4 tbsp butter, melted
1 cup flour
2/3 cup confectioners' sugar
1/4 tsp salt
1/2 tsp vanilla extract

Instructions

- Preheat the oven to 325°F. Lightly grease a 9-inch square cake pan.
- In a medium-sized mixing bowl, beat together the butter, sugar, salt, and flavorings for 2 minutes, until smooth.
- Add the eggs, beating well for at least 3 minutes at medium-high speed.
- Add Marinara sauce, flour and baking soda to the mixture, beating gently to combine.
- Spread the batter in the prepared pan.
- Bake the cake for 30 minutes. While the cake is baking, prepare the topping.
- Mix the topping ingredients together until medium crumbs form.

- After 30 minutes, remove the cake from the oven. Sprinkle the crumbs on top and return the cake to the oven.
- Bake for an additional 15 minutes, until a toothpick inserted into the center comes out clean. Remove the cake form the oven and allow it to cool.
- When the cake is cool, dust it with confectioners' sugar.

If you are gullible enough to follow this recipe, good luck!

Debi, a young lady and one of our most successful sale reps, was getting married. Someone in our office thought a unique wedding gift would be a recipe book featuring recipes contributed by her coworkers. My contribution was the Crumb Cake Marinara recipe. Yuck!

A few years later I was talking to Debi and asked her if she had used any of the recipes in the cookbook. She said she had and had been wanting to try the Crumb Cake Marinara recipe because it looked really interesting.

Debi wondered why I was laughing out loud.

Executive Privilege

As the General Manager of Jason Marketing, I was the boss. Being the boss, could I be late? After all, didn't I have some executive privileges?

The first time my future wife, Teresa, and I had lunch, we went to a nearby Chinese restaurant called Fu Jin. I chose the restaurant because the service was quick, and it was easy to have lunch and get back to work on time, meaning in under an hour.

Teresa and I were seated promptly and handed their large and lengthy menus. I knew what I was going to order before we even left the office, but Teresa did not. She opened the menu and began to look at every option.

The menu was so large that I could not see Teresa and because she was trying to decide what to have, we really couldn't talk. It took Teresa a long time to decide what she wanted to order. Looking at my watch, I realized it had been almost forty-minutes since we left the office and we had not even ordered yet.

We chatted while we waited for our food and as we ate, but I kept thinking about getting Teresa back to work on time. Our office manager wouldn't be happy if she was late, regardless of who she was having lunch with. I wasn't worried about myself getting back on time, because...I was the boss.

I eat fast, so I had finished my lunch and was waiting for Teresa to finish. I knew we were going to be late and I was afraid of the repercussions and gossip when we got back to the office.

Later that day, our office manager walked into my office and I figured that I knew what was coming. I was surprised when she said, "I need to take tomorrow off. I hope that's not a problem."

"Of course not," I replied, feeling she got something for not berating me for making Teresa late.

It wasn't until I took Teresa to lunch the second time and made her late again that our office manager unloaded on me!

51 and 0

Five-foot-five, Ricardo Lopez, also known as "El Finito," was one of the greatest boxers ever. He was the first boxer to retire undefeated in both his amateur and professional careers. His professional record of 51 wins and no losses makes him one of boxing's all-time greats.

How two of my kids and I got to see him defeat Myung-Sap Park as guests of the President of the World Boxing Council is a story worth telling, I think.

Controles Graficos (Graphic Controls), a medical company in Mexico City, was looking for a new supplier for one of their key products. They contacted Jason Marketing, the company Michael and I worked for, and a few weeks later we were on our way to see if this was a legitimate business opportunity.

We made an appointment to visit José Sulaimán, the President of Graphic Controls, at his office in Mexico City. We had a very productive meeting, and it certainly seemed like there was an opportunity to do business together.

As our meeting was wrapping up, I asked Señor Sulaimán if I could use a restroom. He said that I could use his private bathroom adjacent to his office. As I was washing my hands, I noticed a pair of boxing gloves hanging on the wall autographed by Muhammad Ali, the most famous boxer of all times. I wondered how our host came to have such a valuable piece of sports memorabilia hanging in his bathroom!

Going back to our meeting, I asked Señor Sulaimán about the autographed boxing gloves. It was only then that he told us that besides running his medical business, he was the President of the WBC, the World Boxing Council.

Señor Sulaimán and his son, Mauricio, were perfect hosts. We had lunch at their home with their family. That evening, they took us to a hacienda outside of Mexico City for a wonderful dinner. Toward the end of a delightful evening, and after we had enjoyed some excellent tequila, Señor Sulaimán invited us to an upcoming WBC boxing match in Palm Springs.

Michael could not go to the fight, and I thought I might not be able to go because my youngest kids, Drew and Kelly, were scheduled to spend that weekend with me. I called Señor Sulaimán to decline, and he immediately said, "Bring your children. They will love it."

We checked into the Marriott, and I telephoned Señor Sulaimán to let him know we had arrived.

"Please come to our suite and have lunch with us," he said.

Drew, Kelly, Current World Boxing Council President Mauricio Sulaimán and his father the late WBC President José Sulaimán

After lunch, Señor Sulaimán gave each of us our badges for the evening. Kelly looked at her pass that said, "OFFICIAL," and asked what it meant.

"You are an Official," said Señor Sulaimán.

"What does that mean," asked Kelly.

"You can go anywhere you want," said Sulaimán.

"Could I go into the ring," asked Kelly.

"In fact, you could," said Sulaimán. "But please don't. It might cause some problems!"

The highlight of the evening for Drew seemed to be the bikini-clad ring girls that paraded around the ring, holding up a sign that displayed the number of the upcoming round. Sitting in the second row, Drew had a great view of the ladies and seemed to appreciate their role in the fight!

We spent a great evening hobnobbing with boxing's elite and watching Ricardo Lopez knock out Myung-Sap Park in 2 minutes and 22 seconds!

Payback

You may remember me taking my dad's powder blue Ford Fairlane out in the middle of the night and driving 100 miles. If not, go back and read the chapter "A Hundred Miles" OR skip this chapter.

Drew, Kelly, and I were staying at my girlfriend Teresa's house one Saturday evening. About 2:00 a.m., Teresa woke up to use the bathroom and noticed that both of our sons were gone. She woke me immediately.

Not only were our sons gone, but my GMC Safari van was also missing.

I think we only waited about a half an hour with the lights out until Drew and John pulled into the driveway and tried to sneak back into the house. They were quite surprised when we snapped on the lights.

Unlike my escapade years earlier, Drew had a valid driver's license, so he was not doing anything illegal. However, I was pretty pissed-off that he had taken my van in the middle of the night.

"Give me your driver's license," I demanded. I held onto it for about a month before giving it back to him.

A few years later, we learned that the night that we caught Drew and John wasn't the only time they took my van out cruising. But it was the last.

Was this payback for what I had done years earlier…taking my dad's Ford Fairlane out to joyride in the middle of the night?

Choosing the Wrong Door

Standing at the departure gate waiting for my Continental flight to Minneapolis at Newark airport, I was extremely tired. I was standing because I was so tired that I worried if I sat down, I might fall asleep and miss my flight.

"Passenger Mancini, please recheck at the gate," was the announcement.

I had requested an upgrade and getting called back to gate made me optimistic that it had come through.

"I'll give you 1B," said the gate agent. "But you can sit anywhere you want because it looks like you'll be the only passenger in First-class."

A short while later, priority boarding was announced. I walked down the jetway with my roller bag and briefcase and was directed to the aircraft on the right by a gate agent. A flight attendant at the door welcomed me, and after shoving my carry-on in the overhead bin, I grabbed a window seat in the first row. I sat down, buckled up, and closed my eyes.

The loud announcement that the aircraft doors had been closed woke me. A gentleman in the seat next to me said, "You're in my seat, but don't worry about it."

I looked around and was surprised to see that the First-class cabin was almost full.

"Going home to Chicago?" he asked.

My gut told me that something was wrong!

"Wait a minute," I yelled at the flight attendant sitting in a jump-seat next to the cockpit door. "I'm going to Minneapolis."

She quickly picked up the intercom, and I could hear her tell the pilot not to pull back.

"Thirty seconds later and you would have been on your way to Chicago," she said. "Let me see your boarding pass."

The flight attendants disarmed then opened the aircraft door, and one motioned for me to follow her. We faced a closed aircraft door only about 30 feet away. She hustled to the other plane and banged on the door. Through a small circular window in the door, she signaled to someone inside to open the door.

I thanked the Chicago-bound flight attendant profusely as I boarded my flight to Minneapolis.

"You were our only First-class passenger, and I wondered where you were," commented the flight attendant on the Minneapolis flight.

"I guess that I chose the wrong door!"

Laziness Paid Off

Ludlow Technical Products, a division of Tyco International—yes, the corporation that was run by "Deal a Day" Dennis Kozlowski—acquired Jason, the company I had worked at for 27 years. I was happy with the acquisition because my job continued with the new company, and I received Tyco stock options as an incentive to stay on as General Manager.

My new boss was someone who I had known and worked with as a supplier for many years, and I had a great deal of respect for him. I expected life under the new owners would be great!

The previous owners of the company, a father and son, stayed on as paid consultants. A few months after the acquisition, my boss told me that it was time for them to go, and it was my job to ask them to vacate their offices. Telling Harry and Jerry that they had to leave was a difficult task for me because I not only had worked for them but considered them close friends.

My boss instructed me that I should move into the father's office and our Marketing Manager, Michael, should move into the son's office. Both offices were huge and empty because Harry and Jerry had taken their furniture when they left.

We moved our desks in, but that left most of the space empty. Michael was motivated to get his office fully set-up, so he went shopping that same weekend and ordered a sofa, loveseat, coffee table, and end table. The furniture was made to order, and delivery was scheduled five or six weeks out. Michael used his personal credit card to pay for the furniture. I approved Michael's expense report and submitted it to corporate so that he would be reimbursed.

"We don't have sofas and loveseats in our offices. You need to fix this right away," were the instructions from my boss when he saw what Michael had purchased.

"I'll take care of it," was my immediate response. I walked into Michael's office and told him he needed to cancel his order for furniture, which he did. I was glad that I had been lazy and had not taken the time to furnish my office inappropriately.

A few weeks later, a large conference table and eight chairs arrived for my office. Approving my expenses for the purchase, my boss called me and complimented me for not making my office look like a living room! I guess that my laziness paid off!

Karaoke Nights

Working for Jason Marketing, Panasonic had become one of our largest and most important suppliers. In turn, we had become a significant customer of Panasonic's Battery Division. I was the primary point-of-contact at Jason, and that offered me the opportunity to travel to Japan several times to meet with our business partner.

Panasonic was manufacturing a custom 8.4-volt Zinc Air battery exclusively for Jason. Sales were growing rapidly, and Panasonic thought it essential for us to meet in person to discuss the future of the project. I was invited to a meeting at the factory in Japan.

Panasonic booked a business class ticket for me on Japan Airlines, so I started enjoying the complimentary alcoholic beverages as soon as I boarded the flight. Why not? I wasn't flying the plane and would be sitting comfortably for 13 hours.

The evening I that arrived, a group of managers from Panasonic hosted a formal Kaiseki (traditional multicourse) dinner in a historic Japanese home that had become a high-end restaurant. Of course, we sat on the floor, and of course, excellent Saki was served continuously.

After dinner, more Saki was poured, as four elderly ladies dressed as traditional Geisha entertained us. Their singing and playing the shamisen sounded awful to my western ears. But the entertainment was a special surprise offered by my hosts so I must have enjoyed it tremendously.

Finally, after we had all had way too much to drink, I was driven back to my hotel. I was beat! As I was starting to undress, there was a loud knock on my hotel room door.

"Hank San, Hank San, Let's go." It was the other Hank. (His name was Hideo, but whenever Japanese businessmen go to the U.S. for any length of time, they take an American sounding name.)

"Go where?" I asked.

"We go to my bar. Hurry up!"

It was just about midnight, and I was exhausted…the effect of jetlag and many cups of Saki. But I liked Hank and knew that him taking me to "his" bar was a big deal in Japanese business etiquette.

As soon as we entered the bar, there was lots of yelling because everyone in the bar seemed to know Hank and they were happy to see him. (Hank was stationed in New Jersey but apparently returned to this bar every evening he was in Osaka.) When I say everyone in the bar, I mean all 10 people. With Hank and I making 12, the bar was at capacity.

We both drank whiskey poured from a bottle that Hank kept at the bar. (Dozens of whiskey bottles owned by customers lined the wall.) And, of course, as the night progressed, the Karaoke microphone was passed our way.

While Hank was singing a Japanese song, I was going through the list of available songs and found "I Left My Heart in San Francisco." It was one of a few songs in English. You MUST understand that I was pretty

Group at Panasonic Battery Factory in Osaka. Hank is on the left and I am standing next to him

drunk. Otherwise, there is no way in the world that I would be singing "I Left My Heart In San Francisco" in a Japanese bar! (With a similar amount of whiskey, the next night my rendition of "My Way" was even worse!)

I got back to my hotel after 3:00 a.m., too tired to be tired. I didn't sleep well, waiting for my wake-up call at 6:30. Hank met me for breakfast at the hotel at 7:30, before we departed for all-day business meetings at Panasonic headquarters. Business meetings, with much of the discussion in Japanese, while nursing a wicked hangover, was not the most enjoyable way to spend the day.

Two full days of meetings, three nights of drinking, singing Karaoke, and staying out until early morning seemed to be the way my hosts liked to do business. It was a great bonding experience, but it left me exhausted. I slept on the train back to Tokyo, and I slept on the 12-hour flight back to LA, skipping all alcoholic beverages on my flight home and for the next week!

Mr. Behr

I came out of the restroom and was walking by our receptionist's desk when Janett handed me a slip of paper and said a customer wanted to discuss a quote for cables.

Great…an opportunity for new business!

As I was dialing the phone number, my thoughts were on what this opportunity might turn out to be. I guess I didn't hear that the call was answered, "Santa Ana Zoo."

I said that I was returning a call from Mr. Behr.

Laughter erupted both from the person who answered the phone at the zoo but also from the four or five people standing at my office door.

Vestirsi Come un Italiano

Or...dressing like an Italian

We had not intended to spend the morning shopping in Rome for a black shirt for my wife, but we did!

My wife, Teresa, and I were married in 1998, and took a two-week honeymoon, which included four days in Rome. This was before the European Union was formed and each country had its own unique currency. At the time, one U.S. dollar equaled almost 1,700 Italian Lira.

Some of the things we noticed our first morning in Rome:

The cars were all small, and the drivers appeared to be either blind or crazy or possibly both.

Those not driving small cars very fast were driving motorbikes even faster without regard to their safety or the safety of those around them.

Everyone we encountered looked and acted much more sophisticated than we did.

Italians, at least those we saw in Rome, dressed more stylishly than we did.

Nearly everyone—men, women, and children—were dressed in black, as compared to my wife's white top and my yellow Lakers' tee shirt.

To blend in better, my wife wanted to buy a black top. We stopped into the first woman's clothing store we came across and were immediately greeted by several sales ladies speaking in various languages. When my wife replied in English, perfect English became the language of those helping us.

"I am looking for a simple black top," my wife said.

Black tops (they looked like tee shirts to me) started appearing from all directions in the hands of the young and beautiful sales ladies. They were held up in front of my wife so she could see herself in the mirror, and when she had chosen three or four, she was shown into a changing room. Some of the tops were too small and some too large. Each time a size mismatch occurred; it was corrected almost instantaneously.

After more than a half-hour, my wife finally chose the black shirt that she wanted. I paid for it using a credit card, and the sales lady carefully and beautifully wrapped the shirt in tissue paper, secured with a gold-rimmed seal showing the logo of the store. This elegant package was then placed into a large glossy black shopping bag with the logo of the store stamped in gold foil. The packaging was much more sophisticated than our usual red and white plastic Target shopping bags.

Back at our hotel, I looked at the credit card receipt, then at the complementary currency conversion chart we were given when we checked into the hotel. I looked at the amount on the receipt, then at the conversion chart again, then at the receipt again, and then I realized that we had just paid more than $120 U.S. dollars for what looked like a nice black tee shirt!

But my wife looked more like a bella signora Italiana!

My wife and I in Italy with her wearing her new black tee shirt

Greed

I have never considered myself a greedy person, but thinking back on this situation, it looks like I was.

You may remember me mentioning Tyco stock options. When Tyco acquired the company that I worked for in 1997, they wanted me to stay on. As an incentive to stay for at least three years, the company gave me options to purchase Tyco stock at the price that it was when the acquisition closed, which was about $24 a share.

Tyco was on a buying spree, snapping up companies almost daily. This seemed to be what investors wanted because the price of Tyco stock climbed steadily. A third of my options vested each year. That meant that I could sell vested shares and keep any amount above $24. When the price reached $50, I was feeling pretty darn good. If I exercised some of my options for 1,000 shares, I would earn a $26,000 profit! Wow!

My wife was feeling pretty good about Tyco stock and the increasing value of our stock options too. She asked, "When do I get my Porsche?"

Without thinking, I said, "When Tyco stock hits $70."

About six months later, Tyco stock was selling for $68 a share. It had been climbing steadily, and it certainly felt it was a sure bet that it would break $70 within a week or two.

It did not.

News of tax evasion by the president of the company and newly revealed accounting irregularities caused the stock price to plummet. It finally bottomed-out a couple of months later at just under $7.00 a share.

My stock options were worthless, and my wife still does not have a Porsche!

Another Bag of Cash

Earlier I described my experience being responsible for $40,000 worth of $20 bills in a paper bag. That was my bosses' money, not mine. This story is about a smaller amount...a little over $18,000 that was my money and that I wound up carrying in a McDonald's bag.

For several years, Teresa drove a jade-green Lexus LS400 that we had purchased used. It was a beautiful car until Teresa ran into a Porsche parked three houses down on our street.

I will not get into details of the accident except to say that no one was hurt. Our neighbor, Tom, was very gracious and never seemed to hold it against us that my wife nearly totaled his beautiful black Porsche. It was his pride-and-joy to be sure.

The Auto Club (AAA) insured us, and they handled everything wonderfully. Our neighbor's car was brought back to perfect condition after being in the body shop for more than two months. Our insurance company decided to total Teresa's Lexus.

The settlement from the Auto Club was very fair. They offered us several thousand dollars above retail blue book, and we were completely satisfied.

Teresa saying, "I want another Lexus," led us to search online for a low mileage used car. We found an ES330 with about 25,000 miles at a price we could afford at Tustin Lexus. I called to make sure that the vehicle was still available, and we headed out to look at it. After both of us test drove it, we decided to purchase the car. We agreed to a price and signed all the paperwork. With the settlement from insurance and some money from savings, we were paying cash for the car.

But we had a problem. We were not going to receive the settlement from the Auto Club until Monday and needed that money to complete the deal.

"Just write a personal check, and we will hold it until Wednesday," said the salesman. It being Saturday this seemed like a reasonable thing to do. Teresa drove home in her new-to-us ES330.

On Monday, I went to the AAA office in Costa Mesa and picked up an Automobile Club of Southern California check for the full settlement amount. Check in hand, I drove to the U.S. Bank branch that I used in Westminster, about 10 miles away, to deposit the check. I explained to the teller that I had written a personal check on my U.S. Bank checking account and needed the funds from the Auto Club check to be credited no later than Wednesday. Having had an account at that branch for 24 years, I didn't think that would be a problem.

It was!

"We will give you access to $200 today, and you will have access to another $2,000 on Wednesday. It will take about seven business days for the check to clear so you won't have access to the balance until then," said the young teller.

"Why can't you give me the entire amount immediately," I asked.

"Well, we need to be sure the check will clear," was the reply I received.

"This does not make any sense!" I said. "If there were any chance this Bank of America check wasn't good, you wouldn't allow me to take $2,200 of the money! Let me talk to the manager please."

I did not get into an argument with the manager, but left the branch very dissatisfied, with the undeposited check in hand.

My next stop was at the Bank of America branch in Costa Mesa where the check I was holding was drawn. Going into the BofA branch, I explained the situation and said that I needed the funds represented by the check wire-transferred to my account at U.S. Bank.

"OK, Mr. Mancini. That shouldn't be a problem. Just let me have your BofA account number and the transfer will go out first thing in the morning."

I didn't have an account at BofA, and that quickly put the kibosh on that idea. I could open an account, and then I could deposit the check I was holding in my hand into that account. However, rules or policy meant that the wire transfer could not go out until Thursday. Sxxt!

"I need the money in my U.S. Bank account before then. What can I do?" I asked.

"You could cash the check and then deposit the cash into your other account," replied the teller. Great, I thought.

"Because you are completing a cash transaction in excess of $10,000, you'll have to fill out an IRS form 8300 before we can give you your money."

OK...the form was simple. I completed it, handed it to the teller and a few minutes later I had $18,260 in front of me.

"Do you have an envelope that I can put this in," I asked.

"I'm sure that I can find you one," she replied. After a few minutes, the teller came back and apologized. They were out of envelopes, but she had found a McDonald's bag in the break room. Stuffing the cash into the McDonald's bag, I saw that there were two stale French fries in the bottom. It didn't matter!

It took about 30 minutes to drive back to U.S. Bank in Westminster. I grabbed a counter deposit slip, filled it out and took it to the same teller I had hassled with an hour earlier. Handing the deposit slip and cash to the teller, she looked at the amount and then slowly pushed the cash and deposit slip back to me.

"You know that I cannot accept this until you fill out an IRS form 8300, don't you?"

Swear words were appropriate but, honestly, I didn't say a word!

I checked my bank balance the next day, and it showed the deposit credited and more than enough funds to cover the check I had written to Tustin Lexus. I called the dealer to confirm that it was OK to deposit my check.

"Don't worry about it. Our bookkeeper has been on vacation so the earliest any checks will be deposited is next week."

The Colonoscopy

"We're at the end of the line," said the bus driver as he nudged me awake. "Are you OK?"

Over age 50, we are all supposed to get a colonoscopy to make sure we don't have the beginnings of colon cancer. From my experience having the procedure twice, a colonoscopy is no big deal.

That is, the procedure is no big deal. The prep the night before is very uncomfortable, to say the least. Here are a few tips based on my experiences:

1. Go to Costco, Sam's Club, or BJ's and buy a thirty-roll package of your preferred brand of toilet paper. You will need it.
2. Stock the bathroom with several magazines, or even a set of encyclopedias. You will spend a LOT of time there so you may as well have something to read to pass the time.
3. Be prepared to drink what will seem like gallons of a laxative that I thought tasted like lemon-flavored cat piss.

My colonoscopy was scheduled for 6:30 a.m. at Fountain Valley Hospital. I was asked to check-in by 5:30. I didn't want my wife to have to get up so early to take me, so I devised a simple and foolproof plan.

I would drive myself to the hospital, and my wife would come and pick me up when the procedure was finished. (Patients were not released without someone showing up to drive them home.) Later in the day, when the anesthesia had worn off, I would take the bus back to the hospital, pick up my car, and drive home. That was the plan.

I think that my wife brought me home at about 9:30 a.m. and I slept. A few hours later I woke up for something to eat then fell back asleep again. Finally, late in the afternoon, I woke up and felt normal. I didn't feel any of the grogginess that I'd felt earlier, so I thought it was time to get my car.

I walked to the bus stop about a half-mile from our house and got on a bus that went straight down Warner Avenue to the hospital, about 7 miles away. My car was parked close to the bus stop.

"We're at the end of the line," said the bus driver as he nudged me awake. "Are you OK?"

I had fallen asleep. Being woken up, I looked around and had no idea where I was. I also realized that I was the only passenger left on the bus.

I told the bus driver I had intended to get off at Fountain Valley Hospital.

"We passed the hospital about 30 minutes ago," he said. "Just go across the street, and a bus heading back that way will be along in about 10 minutes. Tell the driver to wake you at Euclid if you are going to sleep."

I was successful in staying awake.

I got off the bus at the hospital, picked up my car, and drove safely home. When I got home, my wife asked, "What took you so long?"

He Took Us to a Dump

For the second time in my career, a large, multibillion-dollar company bought the smaller, privately held company where I was happily working. Soon after the deal closed, we hosted nearly continuous visitors from our new owners.

It was routine to take our visitors out to dinner to get to know each other better and build rapport. My boss had been entertaining our visitors several evenings in a row and needed a break. He asked me to take a couple of the higher-ups out one evening.

My boss said, "Ask them what they like and make sure that you take them somewhere really nice. We're going to be working with these guys for years, so I'm counting on you to make a good impression."

Having no idea what these guys might like or where to take them, I asked during a break in a meeting if they had anything in mind.

One said, "We've heard there is some good Mexican food around here. Take us to one of your favorites."

"Do you want fancy or authentic?" I asked.

Both were from the Midwest and said, "There aren't any authentic Mexican restaurants in our area, so someplace authentic would be great."

Nearby Santa Ana is the center of Mexican culture for Orange County. Not more than three or four miles from the office is a small Mexican restaurant that we often went to for lunch. The food and service were great, and it was inexpensive. But while the restaurant was spotless, the decor was dated and showed wear.

Located in an older strip mall, the restaurant is next to a bakery, drycleaners, nail spa, teriyaki place, and liquor store.

Pulling up to the restaurant, one of our visitors asked, "What kind of a place is this?"

"This is authentic Mexican," I replied. "You'll like it."

The tabletops are bare wood, and there are no fancy tablecloths or linen napkins. As soon as we were seated, our waitress delivered salsa and a large basket of warm tortilla chips.

One of the guys ordered a burrito and was shocked when our waitress delivered the nearly one-pound monster to our table. Along with several refills of tortilla chips, each of us had several Mexican beers. To say that we were too full for dessert was an understatement.

The impression that I had was that both of our guests really enjoyed their meal. Certainly, both cleaned their plates. Even more than the food, I thought we enjoyed getting to know each other better, talking about our personal lives for several hours!

When I dropped them back at their hotel, both thanked me for taking them to dinner and for the great choice of the restaurant. I drove home late that evening, thinking to myself, "That went well."

The next morning, I saw our two guests come in and head into my boss's office. Walking in to say good morning, and before they saw me, I heard one of them reply when my boss asked how dinner was, "Hank took us to a real dump last night!"

I guess things did not go as well as I had thought.

2,611 Miles

Several times I flew 5 ½ hours from Los Angeles to Boston, stayed 45 minutes then flew 6 hours back. Was this a crazy thing to do?

Why did I do this, and why did I choose to fly to Boston? Los Angeles to Boston is the longest nonstop flight you can take from LAX within the continental United States. It is 2,611 miles each way. A round trip would earn me 5,222 EQM's (elite qualifying miles).

When I regularly traveled for business, maintaining an elevated frequent flyer status was important to me. It meant that even if I did not receive an upgrade to the front of the plane, I could get one of the best seats in coach and be offered free food and drink during my flights. As the calendar year was coming to an end, I would often find myself in need of additional miles to achieve the status that I wanted on American Airlines.

Selfie of me racking up 2,611 miles flying LAX to Boston

Taking a flight to earn frequent flyer miles is called a "mileage run." It is a pretty common practice among serious flyers. The key to a good mileage run is finding a flight that is both convenient and goes the longest distance for the least cost. Between Thanksgiving and Christmas, I was often able to find a round-trip flight on a Tuesday or Wednesday to Boston for well under $200. Besides being cost-effective, it was an easy, but long, same-day trip.

My wife thought this was somewhat crazy but enjoyed the benefit when we were able to fly business class or first class on vacations.

And my mileage runs were very productive. In-flight Wi-Fi allowed me to get a lot of work done, so my boss considered these flights workdays.

How many times did I make this trip across the country and back the same day? Six times in four years! Was that a crazy thing to do? You decide.

The Most Difficult Time

Most of the other chapters in this book relate amusing incidents in my life, and there have been many. Certainly, the most challenging time in my life was when my wife, Teresa, spent 71 consecutive days in the hospital in 2018.

A year earlier, Teresa's cardiologist had diagnosed her with mitral valve regurgitation and congestive heart failure (CHF). She needed to have her valves repaired…a valve job. Fortunately, one of the experts on robotic, minimally invasive valve repair surgery practiced at our hospital.

Robotic surgery was scheduled for February 9th. On February 8th, a day before surgery, we received a call from the surgeon's office and were told that the specialist was gone and that we would have to find another surgeon! To this day, we don't know what happened to him.

To further evaluate her condition, Teresa's cardiologist did an angiogram and found that two major arteries were clogged. This meant that she would need open-heart surgery. Because of her kidney transplant in 2010, Teresa is immune suppressed. She needed to have her surgery done at a hospital that had a team to manage the care of her transplanted kidney.

Teresa had open-heart surgery on Thursday, March 22, at USC/Keck. We were very relieved when the surgeon told us that the surgery went well with no problems. We would be able to see her in a few hours.

Teresa was in the ICU but looked remarkably good even though she was connected to 11 IV and monitoring lines! She was just barely conscious but recognized us. Teresa couldn't talk because of the trach tube in her throat that was connected to a ventilator to help her breath. We did not stay long Thursday evening because she kept falling back asleep.

Teresa was awake Friday the 23rd. She had been taken off the ventilator, and the breathing tube had been removed late afternoon. Our children, Whitney and John, and John's girlfriend, Katy, were there with me. Teresa was very hoarse and still groggy, but she was talking to us. Before I left the hospital that evening, I kissed her goodnight, told her that I loved her, and she hoarsely replied that she loved me too.

It would be more than a month until she was conscious enough to acknowledge me again.

Driving to the hospital on Saturday morning, I received a call on my cell phone. The doctor said that Teresa had not been getting enough oxygen. A breathing tube, connected to a ventilator, had been put back in her throat. When I got there, she was sedated and unresponsive and would remain in that condition for weeks.

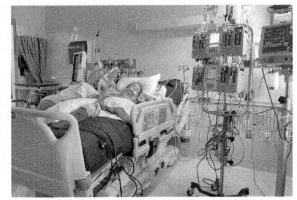

Day after day, Teresa lay in her ICU bed, usually with her eyes wide open staring at the ceiling and often with her arms and legs thrashing. The medical team ran every test possible to try to determine why she was unresponsive. None of the test results pointed to a reason for her condition.

I spent every day at the hospital. I wanted Teresa to know that I was there, even though she did not respond. I also wanted to be involved with her care and understand everything that was being done to help her. Our six kids all visited and our niece Alison who gave Teresa one of her kidney's in 2010 came over from Hawaii twice. Our youngest son, John, and his girlfriend, Katy, were there almost every day. Many of Teresa's good friends came to offer their support.

Being there daily, I got to know the doctors, nurses, and PCT's (patient care assistants) taking care of Teresa. I brought in enlarged photos of Teresa before her surgery and taped them to the wall. I wanted her caregivers to see she had been a healthy and active person. Their care would be key in helping her get back to her "old self."

On April 25, I was on one side of Teresa's bed and Lewis, the PCT, was on the other. We had been watching Teresa and chatting all morning. I commented to Lewis that one of the ways to tell if Teresa was aware of what was going on would be for her to be watching TV.

Lewis said, "Hank, I think she is watching TV!"

I said, "Hi, Honey."

And for the first time in more than a month, she turned her head, looked at me, and smiled! I started crying.

As Lewis talked to her from the other side of the bed, she turned her head and smiled at him, too. When Lewis asked her to wiggle her fingers on her left hand, she did it. This was truly amazing. Even though she had a trach tube in her throat, she was breathing on her own. All her vital signs were good. For the first time in a month, I had confidence that Teresa would recover. Lewis and I high-fived each other!

Alison had flown in from Hawaii and arrived at the hospital later that afternoon. When she greeted Teresa, she got a big smile with Teresa's eyes wide open.

One of the physical therapists made Teresa's bed into a "cardio chair." Teresa was frightened of being moved and sitting up, but her movements were deliberate. The expressions on her face were those of someone who knew what was going on.

We all saw Teresa mouth the words "I want ice." She saw a bottle of water on the side counter and pointed to it and mouthed, "Water."

Unfortunately, with the trach tube in her throat, she couldn't have either. But thankfully, Teresa was alert and seemed to have turned the corner to recovery.

Physical therapy played a more significant role in Teresa's care now that she was able to respond. Clarissa, the therapist that came daily, worked with Teresa to get her to relearn to do simple things like reach with her hand, or kick with her foot. It took several days before Teresa was able to do this, and she was frustrated. We were happy when, out of frustration, Teresa mouthed the "F" word!

Ashley was Teresa's nurse on Sunday, April 29. She was a sweetheart and felt that it would help Teresa's recovery to get her outside to sit in the sun. It took about an hour to get all the equipment set-up for Teresa to leave her ICU room. John, Katy, Alison, and Aly were all there and helped get Teresa into the cardio chair. The group of us wheeled Teresa out of the ICU, into an elevator, outside the hospital, into the sun.

It was very bright, so John put his hat and sunglasses on his mom. We all gathered around her for a photo, which she hates. Minutes later, one of Teresa's oldest friends, Jodi, showed up and that really made Teresa smile. The oxygen bottle was getting low, so it was time to head back into the hospital. Teresa had been outside for over a half an hour, and this seemed to be a significant boost in her recovery.

When I got to the hospital on Monday, April 30, the team was in the process of moving Teresa from the ICU into a regular hospital room. This was a huge step, confirming that she was recovering. Along with moving out of the ICU came increased physical and occupational therapy. One of the goals now was to get Teresa to speak, which required plugging her trach tube with a special one-way valve. This frightened her because it made breathing more difficult. Another goal was to retrain her to swallow so that she could have ice chips, sips of water, and eventually food.

Thursday, May 3, started as a horrible day. I got to Keck at about 9:00 a.m. Teresa had not slept, and that made her both tired and obstinate. She still had the trach tube in her throat and couldn't talk without using her speaking valve, and she wasn't having any part of using the valve this morning.

I was frustrated because Teresa was talking, mouthing words, but I could not understand her. That made her even more frustrated. I finally got it when she mouthed "Leave." And pointed to the door. Very disappointed, I went home.

Later in the day, I was getting ready to head back to Keck when Teresa's nurse called. "Your wife is being transferred to Orange Coast Memorial this evening. The ambulance is scheduled for 7:00 p.m."

I texted everyone that was following Teresa's recovery then headed over to Orange Coast.

I waited at the ER entrance until the ambulance from Keck arrived at about 9:00 p.m. Teresa had been sedated for the move and was drowsy. Once I made sure she was in her room, was being cared for, and left my contact information, I went home. Visiting Teresa in the hospital would no longer mean commuting three or more hours a day.

Teresa spent a month at Orange Coast Memorial. Her recovery could be described as, "Two steps forward and one step back."

She had some very good days and some horrible days. But she got better and better. She went from struggling to drink water to eating soft ground-up foods to eating anything, which allowed the feeding tube in her belly to be removed on May

22. Finally, the trach tube was removed, and Teresa could talk normally.

Friday, June 1, was a day we that had been waiting for since her surgery 10 weeks earlier. Teresa came home!

Sirens All the Way

I was lying on a gurney in the ambulance and overheard one of the paramedics tell the driver, "Use the sirens all the way." We were headed from my home to the Trauma Center at Hoag Hospital. I was very frightened!

The paramedics had arrived at our home about 5 minutes earlier and had quickly determined that the severe chest pains I was experiencing were a heart attack.

My wife and I had just finished breakfast when my back and chest started hurting. The pain that I was feeling was the worst I had ever experienced. It felt like a pile of bricks were stacked on my chest.

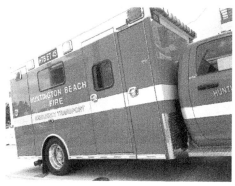

"I think you need to call 911," I said to Teresa.

We arrived at Hoag, and a physician in the ER was waiting. I don't think I was in the ER for more than a few minutes before being wheeled into the Cath Lab. Dr. Levin and his team were waiting for me, and within minutes I was prepped and was undergoing an angiogram.

"One of your arteries is 99-percent occluded," said Dr. Levin. The pain was still severe, but about 10 minutes later it was completely gone.

"The pain is gone! What happened?" I asked.

"We cleared the blockage and put in a stent," said Dr. Levin. "That's what we do. The pain is supposed to be gone."

About an hour later I was moved into a private room on the 9th floor with a fantastic view of the Pacific Ocean. Two days later, I went home.

From the time my wife called 911 until I arrived at the hospital and the blockage was cleared was less than an hour. A subsequent echocardiogram showed no damage to my heart.

I feel truly fortunate for the fast and excellent medical care! I feel even more fortunate to still be here!

Choosing the Wrong Door...Again

No, I didn't board the wrong flight again and I didn't choose the door with a crappy prize on "Let's Make a Deal." I just looked stupid!

Going to a follow-up appointment with my primary care physician after my heart attack, I was a few minutes early. I walked up to the double doors of the office and found a sign that said USE OTHER DOOR with an arrow pointing left. I walked about 30 feet down the hallway to the only other door and tried it. It was locked.

I knocked on the door but got no response. I then banged on the door, but again got no response. Finally, at the top of my voice, I yelled, "I've got an appointment, let me in."

One of the doors to my right, where I first saw the Use Other Door sign opened, and a lady asked, "What's going on? Why are you making such a racket?"

"I've got an appointment, and the sign said to use this door," I replied.

The lady who wondered why I had made so much noise started laughing. "It means to use the left door. The right door is broken."

Checking in at the counter of my doctor's office, the two assistants were both smiling at me. One said, "Well, you certainly gave us something to laugh about this morning."

Swallowing a Stick

This is the last chapter in this book since this story happens in 2019.

Our 9-year-old granddaughter, Layne, has been performing since she was a couple of years old. Her first paid job was modeling children's clothes in the Hanna Andersson catalog when she was two. A very well-known agency represents her, and she is has had small parts in TV commercials and two short films.

Layne's mom, Aly (our oldest daughter), sent a photo of Laynie and me into her agent because she understood they were looking for a "natural" grandfather and granddaughter. I did not know about this until Aly called and said that they wanted Layne and me to audition. And, they wanted us to audition in our bathing suits. I didn't have much of a desire to do this, but if it helped Laynie, of course, I would do it.

The audition was at a casting office on Melrose Avenue in LA. Shortly after we showed up, they asked us to change into our bathing suits and then come into one of the studios. The only one in the studio besides us was a cameraman. He asked us to introduce ourselves to the camera and then for me to pretend to swallow a 30-inch long dowel—aka a stick.

The idea was that I would turn my body so that the camera couldn't see that I was not really swallowing the stick. It would go alongside my mouth and be hidden by my neck and body. While I was doing this, Layne was supposed to show how surprised she was that I could swallow this really long stick. We did four or five takes, and I guess I finally got it right.

A week later, we got a "call back." A call back is a good thing for an actor. It means that they have narrowed the field of acting candidates and want to see you again. This time the audition was on La Brea at an even larger casting facility.

When it was our time to audition, we changed into our bathing suits and went into the studio. There was, of course, a cameraman. But, besides the cameraman, five people were sitting on a couple of couches watching us perform. I asked who all the people were and was told that they were the client. Having six people watch our audition was intimidating.

I must have perfected pretending to swallow the stick because on the first take we got a "thumbs up" and we were told that we could leave, without any other feedback. From what I understand, the most common feedback from an audition is no feedback at all.

Unusual for LA, it was pouring rain. Traffic was terrible, and it took us more than two hours to get home! We had now auditioned twice for this commercial, taking a big chunk of time on two days. I wondered if it would be worth it.

A few days later, Layne's agent called and said that we didn't get the job. I am sure the reason was that my stick swallowing was not convincing enough. I know that Laynie did a great job showing how impressed she was with me swallowing the long wooden stick.

Not being chosen to act in this commercial with my granddaughter surely ended my acting career and is also the end of this story!

The End

This is the end of this book. But as I write this, I am still alive, so there may be more good times to enjoy and more stories to tell.

Having taken 73 years to accumulate these experiences, I doubt whether I will have time to collect enough to fill another book.

Ending this story, I would like to give a little advice to my children and grandchildren.

- Try to be nice to others
- Admit it when you are wrong
- Do things in moderation
- Try to be silly and have fun
- Be thankful for what you have
- Enjoy your life

I wish that I could say that I always followed the advice that I am offering, but often I did not!

I thank my parents for their wonderful example of how to live happily. I also thank them for their love. They have always been there for me and the rest of the family and still are at 91 years old.

About the Author

Hank Mancini retired in 2017, having written technical articles on such captivating subjects as medical cables and connectors for more than a decade. To broaden the appeal of his writing, especially for family and friends, he spent the last two years authoring his first novel, "The Cat That Ate a Thousand Bananas."

Hank and his wife Teresa share six grown children and live in Huntington Beach, California with a dog, a bird, and yes, a cat.

Made in the USA
Monee, IL
27 April 2020